I'LL CARE FOR YOU

I'LL CARE FOR YOU

Linda Fane was in her second year at Bardmore's Hospital when Alan Torringfield was admitted as a patient. Linda had cut herself off from her earlier life, but Alan was a distant relation of hers and also the cause of much of the trouble she wanted to forget. Linda at once saw the threat of complications, as she was on the point of becoming engaged to a young journalist named David Blake, who knew very little of her early background.

I'll Care For You

by

Kay Winchester

Dales Large Print Books
Long Preston, North Yorkshire,
BD23 4ND, England.

British Library Cataloguing in Publication Data.

Winchester, Kay
    I'll care for you.

      A catalogue record of this book is
      available from the British Library

      ISBN   1-84262-444-X pbk

First published in Great Britain by Ward, Lock and Co. Ltd.

Published in Large Print 2006 by arrangement with
S. Walker Literary Agency

Dales Large Print is an imprint of Library Magna Books Ltd.

Printed and bound in Great Britain by
T.J. (International) Ltd., Cornwall, PL28 8RW

Chapter One

I have never liked night duty. It is a world of vast uncanny silences, broken only by the sharp alarm cry of a patient. Vast tracts of darkness, broken by the dim mysterious light over the central table. In that darkness come crises, and a nurse must never, ever, betray her own emotions. I broke that important rule for the first time, on a sultry night in June.

The windows were opened at the tops, but the night was airless. Patients stirred restlessly. Frances Blake, the other student nurse on duty, was at the other end of the ward when I first saw him, in a corner bed previously unoccupied, his legs slung on pulleys to the ceiling, and the old devilish glint in his eyes.

'No!'

The word was wrung from me, and yet it could have been scarcely more than a whisper, a word escaping on a sigh. Not enough for the patient in the next bed to hear, and to look up.

He chuckled softly, and said, 'Hello, nurse.'

Nothing in that. Nothing at all to create

notice. But the look on his white face was enough to set my heart hammering, and as I hurried from bed to bed, until I met Frances at the other end, I wondered how it was I hadn't noticed him before. He must have been dozing when we had come on duty. Perhaps Frances had been at his end of the ward instead of me – I couldn't remember. Or perhaps I had just lost the habit of searching each new face, to see if it was someone I knew, or who had known me in those far-off days before the crash came, two whole years ago.

I don't remember how I got through that dreadful night without betraying myself. Perhaps it was because of the excitement of the haemorrhage in bed No 3, or the quiet death of the sad-eyed young man in No 11, that took my mind off that large, still figure with the slung-up legs, in the corner bed. The nurses' midnight meal came and went, and before I had gone down to breakfast, I realised that I should have no trouble tonight, at least, for he was sleeping. There would be no chance to mention him to Frances, and for that, at least, I was thankful.

Frances Blake and I had started on the same day, we had both been twenty-one at the time, and we had both blundered through our lectures and early exams together during that hectic first year. Somehow we had almost always managed to be on

8

night or day duty at the same time, although not always in the same ward. We were close friends, and I should have told her about the new patient, but I couldn't.

I dreaded waking them in the morning, but when I took his tea, he merely gave me that strange lop-sided smile which I remembered so well; half-devilish, half-threatening. He said nothing until I went to wash him, and then all that I had been dreading came, in his few well-chosen words: 'Linda Fane, I've found you.'

'I should hardly have thought you'd have looked for me,' I said, rather tartly, and keeping my voice down.

'How long have you been here?' he asked, softly.

'Eighteen months,' I told him.

'Don't I have the good luck?' he chuckled.

'I shouldn't think it very good luck to get in this state, just for the sake of running someone to earth who didn't want to–'

'Didn't want to be found by Alan Torringfield?' he took me up. 'Your luck was out. I've been abroad all this time. The first time I came back, what happened but that I got mixed up with a lorry. And look where it's landed me.'

'Haven't you caused enough trouble, for yourself as well as for other people?' I muttered bitterly, as I left him.

I didn't give him a chance to say much

more before I went off duty, and I prayed that he would be out of the hospital before I went on to that ward again.

My only hope was that Frances hadn't realised that there had been an admission whom I knew, but she had seen me talking to him.

'I didn't know you were a fast worker!' she grinned, as we got undressed and prepared to fall into our beds.

I paused on the edge of mine, tempted to tell her about Alan Torringfield. I hesitated, because of her brother David, and the moment was lost.

'Shall I tell Dave?' she pursued, laughing.

I could feel a slow flush mounting up my cheek, and misinterpreting, she burst into peals of delighted laughter before flopping flat on her back and muttering how tired she was.

I hadn't been flushing because of her laughing threat to make David Blake jealous. I had just realised with horror that up till this moment, Alan Torringfield had put David right out of my head.

I couldn't sleep, tired though I was. The hot June sun beat mercilessly down on our side of the hospital block, and despite the dark blind which we had drawn over the uncurtained windows, the light still seemed to seep in, whitely, and penetrate even under our closed lids.

I must sleep, I told myself feverishly. I was meeting David tonight.

When at last I fell off into an uneasy slumber, it was to dream a hideous nightmare, made up of that old life and punctuated with ambulance bells. The casualty ward was on the corner of our block, the nurses' home being built into the hospital building. I woke at two-hourly intervals, sweating with terror, only to fall asleep almost at once to dream more bad dreams.

David Blake was dark like Frances, with glossy black hair carefully brushed to flatten out the deep waves. A square face, with a firm chin, and a pair of honest dark brown eyes. When he met me, he always seemed to scan my face anxiously, and I had the uneasy feeling that he knew there were things I had never told him.

'You look washed out, Linda,' he greeted me. 'Bad day?'

'Oh, no, we're off nights for a while,' I breathed. 'What are we going to do?'

'Well, pictures? Or a walk in the park? It's hot to be inside, isn't it?'

I agreed, but I didn't want an evening session of talking. I knew my David. He'd been probing a little lately. I had expected it. According to Frances, his intentions being honourable, he had every right to know a bit more about me than she did, which was – beyond what she knew of me in hospital –

11

practically nothing.

Once in the green stillness of the park, with the daylight beginning to lose its glare as the sun prepared to set, I began to feel more rested.

We sat and smoked and talked, in a long avenue of trees, our seat in one of many niches in a huge thick hedge, so that apart from a few passers-by, we were cut off from the grey dust and never-ceasing noise of the London streets.

David said, 'This nursing racket's killing you, Linda. Why don't you throw in the towel?'

'Are you just urging me to do what you consider the sensible thing, or are you asking a straight question?' I smiled.

'Both, perhaps.'

'Dave, I'm all right,' I said, quickly. 'Don't be misled by my pale skin. Fair people always look washed out in this game, and the heat and everything. I'll be all right.'

'Just what does nursing mean to you?' he asked suddenly.

'If I said "everything", you wouldn't believe me. If I said "justification", you'd think I was being smug. If I said "escape", you'd be shocked. What *do* you expect me to say, David?'

'The truth,' he said, staring into my eyes.

'Well, perhaps it's a bit of all three. I don't know.'

'Linda, I know so little about you. Why did you take it up in the first place? Where were you when you decided?'

I could feel my face getting frozen, as it always did when people asked me questions, even David.

He went on, without having apparently noticed, 'Frances took it up because she couldn't think of anything else she'd like to do. We didn't think it the proper spirit at home, but Mother said we were to leave her alone. Now she seems actually to enjoy it.'

'And you find that hard to believe?' I prompted.

He nodded. 'Frances looks for fun in everything, and if she enjoys nursing, I can't believe that it'll last. Not from what I know about it.'

'Why did you take up writing, David?' I countered.

He was suddenly fierce, intense. 'Because of something inside me, that drove me to it, ruddy fool that I am! I'd have done far better if I'd gone into a factory or something.'

I leaned forward, interested. 'Then you don't like writing?'

'Like it?' He laughed. 'I don't know. I just do it because I have to. It's not what I would have chosen. Can you imagine what a lonely existence it is, sitting in my bedroom all day, pounding a typewriter, never knowing anyone else who writes, never having anyone else to discuss it with?'

'And yet you'll go on doing it, David?'

'I'll go on doing it,' he said. 'Because it's what I'm fit for. And I'm making money. Good money.' He leaned forward a little. 'But Linda, I don't think you are fit to be a nurse, and it isn't good money. Better than it was, but not good. Why do you go on?'

'Would you like me less if I chucked it?'

'No. I'd think you'd done the right thing,' he said.

'What would you suggest I did, by way of a living?' I asked idly, because I couldn't tell him that although nursing had been just a good sound profession in my estimation when I took it up, I had since come to the startling conclusion that I had a passion for nursing. I didn't mind the drudgery of it, nor the exhausting business of getting up early. I didn't mind the sight and smell of blood, or any of the other sights and smells that had turned away many student nurses even in the brief time I had been at Bardmore's Hospital. And I found an increasing appetite for all the things we were learning, day by day. I loved watching hands: anyone's hands. Surgeons', sisters', even the nurses' only slightly above me, if they were doing a job I hadn't tried. It was all new and absorbing.

But I couldn't tell David that. I couldn't

find words to talk about myself, nor could I manage to explain away anything I felt or experienced. Above all, I distrusted anything which might lead to a confidence, because confidences had an uncanny knack of shooting backwards, into the past, treacherously leading to the unearthing of things better left covered.

My question was an unfortunate one. David pounced on it.

'Be my wife,' he said.

Afterwards, when I thought about it, I realised that it must have cost him a lot to say that, for he was a shy person. He must have rehearsed it in a thousand ways, and still jumped in at the opportunity I had provided.

'Oh, David!' I cried, distressed, and shocked to find a stricken look on his face.

'Mother says you're not strong enough to stay the course alone,' he stammered, 'and I don't suppose anyone expects Frances to last out the full three years. She's only hanging on by the skin of her teeth as it is. I wouldn't like to think of you there alone, and nowhere to go—'

'Is that why you're proposing to me, David?'

He whitened.

'Linda, you must know how I feel about you. I haven't made any secret of it. My dear, I could tell you in flowery language

15

how I feel, but I wouldn't. I'm a writer, and words are my stock-in-trade. It wouldn't ring true. Besides, you're such a calm person. Sometimes you're even remote. I don't even know if it would embarrass you to hear me talk like it. I can only say that you're ... the only one ... for me.'

The bright light of the day seemed suddenly to fade. I saw Alan Torringfield in that corner bed, with his legs slung up, and I felt my heart thudding as I recalled him. My heart had no business to behave like that. It wasn't fair that he could come back like this, just to-day of all days.

David said, 'You've never seemed to have any other friends. You've spent all your spare time with me, so far as I know, Linda, there isn't anyone else, is there?'

I shook my head, bewildered. I couldn't say no. Not while Alan Torringfield was lying there. I couldn't say yes, either. I wasn't in love with Alan. But I didn't understand what emotion it was that he could produce in me, to make all this turmoil. That was the way it had always been. I couldn't even begin to think about David in that way, while Alan was so near.

'David, I don't want to get married or be in love or have any such complications while–'

'I'm not asking you to have complications,' David said sharply. 'I happen to be

16

in love with you.'

He could say it easily enough when he was angry. It made me smile, and it lessened the tension.

'David, I've got another eighteen months. Leave me to get through it somehow, and then when I've done that, well–'

'Well, what, Linda?'

'Well, if you still feel the same way about me, ask me again then,' I said, breathlessly.

He shook his head, slowly, and there was a look in his eyes that I didn't understand.

'I've got the offer of a newspaper job in the Midlands,' he said. 'I'd made up my mind to turn it down. I shouldn't be able to see you very much. I think I'll take it after all.'

Sharp disappointment must have shown in my face, for he watched me curiously.

'It's selfish, I know,' I said. 'I'll miss you so horribly. But if you want to take it, and it's going to be a good thing for you–'

'You don't really mind if I go?'

'I have no right to, David.'

He took my shoulders in his big strong hands, and shook me a little. 'Linda, if I could only get beyond that awful barrier! I don't think you mean to hide things, but if only you'd come out in the open with them.'

'What does that mean, David?' I asked frigidly.

'Linda, we don't know anything at all about you, and we've known you – you've been coming regularly to our home – ever since you and Frances paired up at the hospital. We don't know if you have any people, or if you're quite alone. We don't know even where you lived before you went to Bardmore's. Nothing at all about you. Just as if a wall was built between your early life and your twenty-first year.'

'Don't you think I'd have told you if I'd wanted to?' I burst out. 'Do you think it matters, if I haven't told you? Don't you realise that it just isn't important, and that's why I've said nothing? Nothing in my early life could possibly affect you or your family, David. You know everything about me since we met.'

'Do I?' He searched my eyes, his own unhappy and pleading. 'Do I? I wonder. Linda, I love you, my dear. My family love you. Every one of them – Mother, Dad, Frances, young Barbara and John – they all love you as if you were one of us. They hope you'll be one of us some day. But they all feel hurt and disappointed that you haven't trusted us so far as to tell us–'

'It isn't a question of trust, David. It just didn't matter. You know me – I never say anything that doesn't matter much – I hate talking for the sake of talking.'

'I used to think that,' he said, slowly. 'But now I feel it isn't so. I think you've got something to hide.'

'Why should I?' I flared, my face flaming. Fear as well as anger jostled together. I could bear to put off David's proposal. I wasn't ready for a proposal from anyone. I couldn't bear to lose the very real friendship his family had offered me. I had had enough of losses, and not so long ago. That icy loneliness loomed up again, and I was terrified.

'I've given you a chance to talk to me tonight, and you wouldn't. I asked you if there was someone else, and you denied it.'

'There isn't anyone else!'

'Isn't there? Frances got home just before I came out to meet you,' David said, in a curious flat voice. 'She's full of a new patient, who was in the news a couple of years ago. It was a nasty scandal. A man named Alan Torringfield.'

My heart lurched. That was one of the things that always made me angry, about Frances. She always blurted things out when she was excited, and then she was sorry afterwards. It didn't make any difference. She was never cured.

'What of it?' I asked, through frozen lips.

'I heard her telling Mother that you were talking to him on the ward. She seemed to think you knew him.'

Chapter Two

Through the star-spangled dusk of that June night I could see pictures of the past. A thousand things leapt to my mind to say to David. They must necessarily be brief, and again I decided that I couldn't risk it. No words, reduced to précis form, could ever come near to accurately portraying my side of that dreadful business. The wrong impression was the last thing I wanted him to receive.

'Yes, I do know him,' I said, levelly. 'What of it?'

David evidently hadn't expected that.

'He doesn't seem the sort of person I'd expect you to know, Linda,' he said, at last.

'One can't choose one's acquaintances. However undesirable they may be, one can't snub a patient. I expect Frances told you that I only exchanged a few words with him. Does it matter?'

He looked angry. 'You make me feel such a fool, Linda. Ultimately, everything you say finishes up with the question: does it matter?'

'Well?' I murmured, and smiled propitiatingly.

'Things *do* matter,' he muttered savagely. 'It matters very much that you should know a man like that, however slightly, and I don't know about it. Can't you see? I want you to be my wife, and I want peace of mind. How can I have that peace of mind, if I feel that you know people that I've never heard of? How can I have any confidence in you if I remember too often that there's a whole lifetime that you never even let me peep into?'

I knew what he meant, and in my heart I knew he was right. I ought to tell him, or ... give him up. I didn't want to do that. Neither did I want to lift the veil and let him look backwards, beyond my entry into the hospital, and Frances' life.

'Linda,' he urged, desperately, 'tell me just a few things, dearest, just to show that you trust me, and need my friendship. Darling, if you don't need my friendship, let's not go on.'

'I *do* need it,' I found myself whispering.

'Say that again,' he said, a wonderful smile spreading over his face.

'I *do* need it,' I began, and he took me into his arms.

It was comfort I needed most then, no love-making. I slid my mouth away from his, and buried my face in his shoulder. The strength of his arms gave me assurance. He was so good, so honest. It was my terror that

I should hurt him.

'David,' I said, in a muffled voice, 'one day I'll tell you lots of things – everything, perhaps. But not now. And David, can you bear to hear the truth of how I feel about you?'

'I want just that,' he said, his mouth pressed against my hair. He loved my hair, and for him I always went without a hat, though I didn't care for the idea much. He said he adored the way the soft deep waves sprang from my forehead, and finished in thick, tight curls. Lucky for me that it curled naturally, for we got precious little time in hospital to fool about with waving and setting.

'I want the truth, and don't pull any punches,' he repeated, thickly.

'David, I couldn't bear it if I lost you,' I said, hopelessly aware of his grip tightening on me. 'I don't know if that's being in love. Until I know, I don't want to do anything about it. But I don't think I could bear it if you weren't there ... always. Selfish, isn't it?'

'Is it?' he jerked. 'Blest if I know the difference between that and being in love. It isn't all beer and skittles, you know. I don't go for the trimmings. You'll get no romance under the stars from me, Linda. I know you're the one, and there the thing rests. Don't you know if it's ... me?'

I shook my head and pulled away from him. 'No, I don't know. I only know I want your friendship.'

It was unsatisfactory, and I knew it.

'All right,' he said, after a while, and lit a cigarette. 'At least tell me one or two things, that can't possibly matter. Have you got any family?'

I hesitated, and he noticed it.

'David, if you start asking things, it won't stop,' I said, urgently.

'Well, what's wrong in admitting if you've got parents or haven't?' he flared. 'Why make such a mystery of it all?'

'All right, I haven't,' I said, sullenly.

He wanted to know, inevitably, if my orphan state was recent, and there the trouble started.

'No. I was born like it,' I said, tautly. 'In a Foundling Home. I don't know who my parents were.'

He said, flushing, 'I don't want a yarn pitched. If you don't want to tell me any more, say so, right out. I'm not such a fool as to believe a speaking voice like yours came out of an orphanage.'

'Voice culture can be acquired. You asked for the truth and you got it,' I said, and I knew that for some reason he was suddenly convinced. The tight silence seemed unbreakable.

I watched the effect of my disclosure on him, funny, that. Almost everyone who has had a decent home background flinches just

23

a little from the stigma of that word 'foundling'. I grinned.

'That makes a difference, doesn't it, David?' I asked, softly, watching the conflicting emotions on his face.

'Yes,' he agreed, roughly. 'It makes me feel even more tender to you. Now I want you to belong to me quicker, so that I can give you all the home background you've never had.'

Unshed tears burned in my eyes.

'Don't do that!' I said, sharply. 'I don't like pity.'

'Oh, Linda, Linda, why are you like this? Why hurt yourself so much? Do you think that any of us, any one of my family, wouldn't love you even more, knowing that?'

'I thought it was understood that anything I told you was in confidence?' I asked quickly, sharply almost.

'In confidence? What, when the hospital authorities know it already, and it's on their files for anyone to see?' he smiled, fondling my hand.

I snatched my hand away. 'They don't know,' I said, angrily.

He frowned. 'You didn't put that on your Application Form?' he asked.

'Why should I? I was of age, remember.'

'But your address?'

'My digs, of course. I answered everything that was required of me.'

'But what did you say about the trade or

profession of your father?' he pressed.

'You see?' I cried. 'You can't leave well alone. One thing will lead to another. I simply said I didn't know much about my parents, but I gave them all details about the people who brought me up, and that I'd left them and was now on my own. It seemed to me that all the hospital authorities wanted to know was that I genuinely wanted to be a nurse.'

He didn't believe me. I could see that.

'They also want to know what education a girl has,' he reminded me. 'You're not the product of a Foundling Home.'

I was tired of the inquisition. I flung caution to the winds. 'No, you're right. Someone finished me. The combined staff of Adelaide Towers.'

After a shocked silence, David said, 'Adelaide Towers is, I believe, one of the most expensive boarding schools in the country.'

'That's right,' I said, brightly.

'And the girls come from country estates and–'

'And places like Marleigh Park,' I finished.

I wished I hadn't said that. I hadn't had the luxury of giving a confidence for so long, that it was like old wine: it had gone to my head. I looked away from him quickly. I couldn't bear the hurt in his face.

Finally, he threw his cigarette away, almost unsmoked, and thrust his hands deep into his pockets.

'I wish we could turn the clock back, Linda,' he said wearily. 'To just long enough ago where I asked you if you knew Alan Torringfield.'

I waited. I knew what was in his mind.

'So that, instead of all that, all those unwilling answers to my questions, you could have said: "Yes, I knew him. I spent my childhood at Marleigh Park, and I couldn't help knowing him. Couldn't help getting mixed up in that filthy business two years ago." It would have been easy enough to say, wouldn't it, Linda? But since you didn't say that, I suppose it wouldn't have been the truth. You knew very well what you were doing, didn't you?'

'Does it matter?' I asked, slipping back to my favourite line of defence.

'Yes, it matters very much,' he said, getting up.

We walked in silence, to the place where we usually waited for our bus, to take us back to David's home for supper.

'Tell Frances I got a headache and went back early,' I said curtly, and running across the road, dodging other traffic, I hopped on a passing bus in the opposite direction. I didn't want to go back to Bardmore's any earlier than I need have, but it was the first place I thought of, as a retreat from David's hurt and accusing dark eyes.

26

I didn't see David for some time after that. There was plenty to do in my spare time, by way of lectures and private struggles with textbooks. We weren't supposed to have much pleasure. I remember being told, on my first day at the hospital, that any time we had away from the wards was for study, eating and sleeping. Nothing else. Frances was finding the studying much more difficult than I, and something of a barrier came between us after that fateful day in June. We worked together on the wards, and we studied together and went to lectures together. We still slept together, but there was a difference; we spent little leisure together outside the hospital. A lot of the fun had gone out of our friendship, and it was some time since I had been to her home.

I, being obsessed with the idea of David and that last meeting, wondered if he had told Frances what had passed between us, but decided that of all people, David wouldn't do that.

And then one day I realised what was really the trouble, Frances said awkwardly to me.

'Do you still loathe Gordon Evans?'

I looked up in surprise. Gordon Evans was a houseman. Too good-looking, too sauve, and altogether too sure of himself for any student nurse's comfort. Frances and I had made a pact about him, long ago. He had been responsible for Matron's getting to hear of our very first scrape, and she had been unduly watchful of us both ever since. All the staff nurses were silly over him, because of his beautiful blue eyes and his bedside manner, and from every angle we had agreed in the past that it was wise to give him a wide berth.

'Of course I do,' I said.

'Oh, hell, that's torn it,' Frances said.

'Why has it?'

She scuffed her shoe awkwardly, and said: 'Well, the fact is. I don't.'

'Oh, I see.'

'Don't say it like that,' she protested, flushing. 'It's fair and square and above-board.'

'It may be from your side,' I said, scathingly.

'He isn't what everyone says he is,' she protested.

'Well, if you're going to waste any more time on defending him, you'd better find someone else to waste it with.'

'Don't be nasty, Linda,' she said, in an altered tone. 'I was going to ask you to do something for me. I mean, we are still friends, aren't we?'

'Nothing's changed, so far as I am aware,' I said, frigidly. 'But if it's to do with that skunk Evans, well, I don't know.'

'Things have changed,' Frances protested. 'Ever since that night you saw Dave, and he went away.'

Her eyes were bright with curiosity, but not very much hope of being enlightened. She knew me well.

'They haven't changed so far as I'm concerned,' I said, giving the last once-over to the patients' milk and cocoa trolley and preparing to wheel it out.

'Then will you do something for me? It isn't much.'

'What is it, Frances?'

'Only let me in when I get back tomorrow night.'

I stared at her, and she had the grace to blush.

'Heavens, Linda, I don't often ask a favour. It's just that I'll be back after the door's locked, and I wouldn't ask anyone else to do it.'

'You're getting a late-night pass?' I breathed. It was the first time one of us had done that without telling the other, or indeed both getting the same pass, for a mixed party.

'I would have told you, but you seem so keen to spend every minute you get swotting,' she said. 'It's a dance at the Walpole Hotel.'

'The Walpole,' I murmured. 'Have you got a new dress, then? You'll need it, at that place!'

'Yes, I have. Daddie bought me one recently. I'd have shown it to you, only–'

'I know, I was studying too hard to be interested in new clothes,' I said, shortly.

I was desperately afraid of a quarrel, and so I shoved the trolley on its way, leaving her. In effect, I suppose I had promised to let her in. I don't remember what else I said about it, but I got the hazy idea that she was to be let in by dropping off the fire escape on to a small balcony outside an empty private ward. Just the sort of thing Frances would think up for ending an evening's revelry.

As I gave out mugs of cocoa and milk, my thoughts flew to David, and the fact that he had not written to me since he had gone away. From David, it was an easy step to Alan Torringfield, who had, as far as I knew, recovered from his accident and gone. I had been lucky. I had not been detailed to go back to that ward again, and so I had escaped him. But he knew where I was.

I faced the fact. I was glad that there was so much studying to do for my second year exam. It kept me within the bounds of the hospital, where no one could touch me. I was literally afraid to go out in broad daylight, in case I found him waiting there.

I saw Frances getting ready for her evening out, when I came off duty next day. Again for the first time, our duties had been shifted, and she had different hours to mine. It gave me a feeling of uneasiness, and yet I had known that we were having extraordinary good luck in managing to wangle duties and passes together for so long. Now the break had come. We probably wouldn't be able to get back to that happy *au pair* state, even if we wanted to.

Even if we wanted to. I found myself thinking of that later, with sadness. We had drifted apart so rapidly, since the advent of Alan Torringfield.

Oddly, she seemed to be thinking of the same thing. Radiant, after a bath and a brisk extra brushing of her black, gleaming wavy hair, she slithered into a pale lilac velvet dance dress and hesitantly twirled round for me to see the effect.

I sat on my bed and nodded.

'How do I look? Lousy?'

'Lousy,' I agreed solemnly, and we both burst out laughing. And then we stopped laughing and eyed each other in embarrassed fashion. I ought to have made her shake on it, tell her that it was the same as always, but something stuck in my throat. I couldn't, and of course, she was always just a shade wary of that remote manner of mine.

'Who's the beau?' I asked, idly, thinking how lovely she was, with that matt ivory complexion of hers, and the finely moulded mouth, so like David's in its shape, yet more inclined to quiver with laughter than to move softly with tenderness. She had a turned-up nose, too, and a shade of impudence about her loveliness which was very fetching. I helped her on with the exquisite evening coat of deeper purple lined velvet, and was ready for her answer.

'Gordon Evans,' she said, airily.

All the warmth went out of our conversation. I sat down on the bed, and I could feel my face growing frozen with hostility.

'You promised!' she flared. 'You said you'd do it for me! You can't back out now, just because you don't happen to like my escort!'

'You should have said at first who it was going to be,' I said, with anger, nevertheless, but a quieter anger than hers.

'Wouldn't you have done it for me?'

'I don't think I would, Frances.'

'I thought not. Well, it's my business who I go out with, and I think if you're supposed to be my friend, you ought to help me, whatever you think of my choice of escort.'

'You fool!' I suddenly exploded. 'We're in our second year. Do you want to get kicked out before you finish training? You know what Matron thinks about students who philander with housemen.'

'And you know what she thinks of people who bury nasty scandals with patients,' she flared back at me.

We faced each other, both bristling.

'What exactly does that mean?' I

32

demanded, in an icy quiet tone that surprised even myself, for I felt like shouting at her with every ounce of strength in me.

'You know what I meant. That Torringfield man. Everyone knows about it.'

I considered that point. 'Everyone knows about what?' I asked her.

'Everyone knows about the old scandal. They read it in the papers,' she amplified.

'And do they know enough to feel they can connect anyone in particular with it?' I gritted.

'I haven't rushed around and told everyone, if that's what you mean,' she said, with flaming cheeks.

'I wouldn't, if I were you. You might be jumping to the wrong conclusions, Frances.'

She hesitated, and I could see that it was on the tip of her tongue to ask me to tell her if I really had any part in that old story.

I forestalled her. 'And don't think that I'm going to favour you with an inside story either. It's my business.'

'Is that what you told my brother David?' she asked, coldly.

'That also is my business.'

'And mine!' she said, her anger rising. 'I don't care how you treat me, but don't try any of your rotten tricks on my brother. He's too decent to be treated like you've—'

'Like I've what?' I took her up, but she wouldn't finish. I could guess, anyway. Like you've treated other men, she was going to say.

'Forget about letting me in,' she said, gathering up her gloves and tiny silver lame evening bag.

At the door, she hesitated, and looked at me. I wished I could unfreeze my face, but I couldn't. The best I could do was to say thickly, 'Don't be an ass. I'll do it.'

Funny, how old friendships stick, in the atmosphere of hospital. It is, I sometimes feel, an alliance made because of the health line. We who are well, cling together, and those on the other side are those who are not well, and dependent on us. We scrap among ourselves, but ultimately we cling. There are even superstitions about breaking friendships in student days. I could no more have broken with Frances than she could possibly break with me. I knew it, and I think she did, too.

I was on night duty, and I don't think I had really realised what I had taken on until it got near the time for Frances to come back. It was after one in the morning, and about my time to go down to nurses' supper. The staff nurse was to take over my ward while I went, and on the way I was to nip down the side corridor which led to the empty private ward, open the window for Frances, and nip out again to see if the coast was clear for her to skate down to the nurses' hostel wing. She'd be all right if Night Sister didn't change the time of her round – as she sometimes did, with disconcerting results.

All went smoothly until 12.25 when one of those unexpected crises happened. I was alone in the ward, Staff Nurse being down at supper already, when a haemorrhage occurred. Staff Nurse was recalled and Night Sister fetched. In all, it put back my supper nearly half an hour, and I could hear it was raining.

I was sweating by the time I got off at last. I literally ran down the corridors, and wrenched open the door of the empty ward. As I got to the window, a voice from the bed electrified me.

'Don't open that window, nurse. The rain's coming this way.'

I stood for a second, frozen to the spot. My luck was dead out. The room was occupied, and the balcony outside was empty. What was worse, far worse, I recognised the voice of the patient in the bed. Alan Torringfield.

Chapter Three

'What are you doing here?' I found myself muttering angrily, as I sped over to his bedside. Chagrin filled me. I could still, it seemed, forget I was a nurse, in the heat of the moment. Eighteen months wasn't enough to instil that iron restraint, the absence of which betrayed the student status of the nurse.

'Come here, come here,' he murmured, and gripped my wrist. 'Now then, listen. Your pal's in, safe and sound, and mighty ungrateful she was about it, too. Pretty little piece, though!'

I gave a sharp intake of breath. 'How did she–' I began, and bit my lip. A patient had no business to know the things we got up to when we should be safe in the hostel.

'I let her in,' he said calmly. 'I never could bear to see a pretty girl outside in the rain,' and he laughed, the old tormenting laughter which still made me ache to slap him good and hard.

'You had no business to be out of bed,' I stormed.

'And you two had no business to be using a private ward for a secret entrance after

36

hours,' he said, calmly.

'What are you doing in here, anyway? You were in Ward C5,' I said, resentfully.

'I was discharged as fit – from the effects of the accident,' he chuckled. 'Good healing flesh. Strong constitution.'

'Then what are–' I began, but he cut me short.

'–doing in here?' he finished. 'Your luck's out, isn't it, Linda? I had a bout of the old trouble (you wouldn't know about that, a bit before your time!) and I got a private ward, for observation purposes, you understand.'

I forgot about my supper time. I lost my meal eventually, for by the time I had finished talking to him, I should have been back on duty. Intrigued, I pursued the point. 'Why this hospital? I can understand your being admitted after the accident, since you apparently happened to be in this district. But why come back for medical treatment?'

'Ah, I know what you're thinking, but don't flatter yourself, Linda. I didn't come back for love of you. I came back because I was impressed with the treatment I received here before.'

'Liar!' I spat at him.

'It always was your spirit that I admired,' he said, reminiscently, and resisted my struggles to break free, with surprising strength. 'It's true, however.'

'No, Alan, you came back to annoy me. To frighten me. I know you of old. With all the nursing homes in London, did you have to choose this hospital? No, that won't do.'

'Nursing homes? Me? I'm broke, my dear. Did you ever know me to be otherwise?' he smiled, and in the dim light from the corridor, he searched my face for embarrassment, and found it, to his delight. 'You prefer not to remember the old days? I thought not.'

He was a strong man, and quick. Before I realised it, he had pulled me down, and held my head while he kissed me, that same old way of kissing, that, to my shame, left me weak and spent and gasping, and unable to break away.

He was breathing quickly, too, but he let me go eventually. I imagine he was furious with himself, that he could still experience the old wave of emotion. He liked to feel that no girl meant very much to him, and that kissing was nothing more than a pleasant pastime.

I fled from his room without a backward glance.

I was hungry, cross, and more disturbed than I cared to admit. A nurse should be able to manage a patient, and not let anything like that happen, no matter how strong he is.

I went about my duties through the night,

until the nurses' breakfast came round, with half my mind on my work, half my mind on the subject of Alan. How he got that empty private ward, I didn't know, unless the general wards were so full that they were using them as overflow. As to what his 'old trouble' was, I would have given a lot to know, but I dared not ask anyone.

As it happened, the nurse on duty was talking about him at breakfast. I caught the lowered tone as she mentioned that old newspaper case, and could only hope that she didn't recall my name having been mentioned.

'What's the matter with him now, Jean?' one of the nurses asked, laughing a little. Everyone who came into contact with Alan liked him, despite the vague feeling everyone got that he was something of a black sheep. I sometimes think the black sheep get more consideration and affection because of that doubtful condition. A kind of protectiveness towards them, as with the underdog.

'He thinks he's gastric,' Jean laughed.

'He thinks?'

There was a general laugh, and the talk shifted to the other gastrics on the general ward.

'What's he in a private ward for?' someone else asked. 'He must be special.'

'There isn't a thing wrong with him, my

dear, but he said he's in pain, so we're making the usual tests. Besides, we could hardly refuse to take his good money for a ward that isn't in use. But just you wait till a rush of bad cases turns up. He'll be kicked out in no time.'

My face scorched and I prayed that no one would think to look at me. Happily for me, I rarely joined in these meal-time conversations, so that my silence didn't seem odd. I could have told them that there was nothing wrong with Alan, despite his assertion that his trouble was an old one. He had wangled a way back for some reason best known to himself, and it concerned me.

The next night I found him walking down the corridor. He had evidently found out the time I was due to go down to first meal.

'You've no business to be out of your ward,' I hissed at him.

'If I can't get attention, it seems I'll have to look after myself,' he said, mildly.

'You'll aggravate your condition if you're really suffering from something,' I said, furiously. 'Get back to your room. I'll call your nurse.'

'I'll go back,' he agreed, meekly, 'Linda!'

'I can't stop now. I'm on my way to the dining-room.'

'*Linda!*' he said, and there was almost menace in his voice.

I swung round and waited. I believe I had

known all the time what was to be the end of all this.

'Linda, I've been talking to one or two people. Seems this is a pretty strict hospital.'

'No more than most,' I said, curtly. 'What d'you want?'

'To be where we were, you and I, when everything got mucked up,' he said, simply.

'You're mad! Just as if I'd go back to being that sort of fool,' I gasped.

'You'd be more of a fool if you didn't,' he said, quietly. 'You see, I might feel disposed to see that Matron got to hear of–'

'Come back into your ward,' I snapped. 'I can't risk being seen talking to you here.'

He let me help him back into the small darkened room, and stood silently while I helped him off with his dressing-gown and got him into bed. He didn't touch me. He just waited.

'Alan,' I burst out at length. 'Let me be … le me *be*. I've gone through so much since that old affair. I've tried so hard to put it all behind me. It hasn't been easy. Every day, watching, being on my guard, praying no one would find out who I was. I wanted this career so *much*.'

'Why?' he asked, interestedly.

'I *want* to nurse people,' I said, intensely.

'I can't believe it,' he said, at length. 'The last time I saw you, you were wearing ermine and sable, and, let me think, a blue

41

satin gown encrusted with seed pearls; you smelt good and you had as much ice round your neck as you could carry. Don't tell me you like wallowing in blood and bedpans. No, Linda, that won't do.'

I had forgotten that that was the last time he had seen me. I thought of that evening, and a wave of homesickness flooded me with an intensity that frightened me. I thought I had managed to put all that out of my system.

'Ever see Aunt Berenice?' he asked softly.

My throat was full of a lump that wouldn't go down, and my eyes pricked and burned. I shook my head. I couldn't answer.

'You see?' he said, in a low voice. 'You want to go back. You want the old life so badly that it hurts. When you go back on your ward, have a good look round you. Ask yourself how long it will last, even if I don't speed things up for you. As I shall, you know, if you don't do as I – er – suggest.'

'Leave me be, Alan,' I tried again. 'You don't want *me*. It's just that you can see that I'm fixed and happy, and you want to mess it all up again.'

'Don't I want you? Think again, Linda. Did I ever waste my time over something I didn't want?'

I could hear footsteps clap-clapping along the corridor. 'Got to go,' I gasped.

He grabbed my wrist. 'What's it to be?'

With despair in my heart, I said, 'All right,' and fled. Alan's nurse was coming along. She looked curiously at me and asked sharply what I was doing in there.

'Found your gastric in the corridor. Just got him back to bed,' I said, and ran.

When I saw Frances again, I wondered what her reaction would be. Did she think I had decided against letting her in, after having promised? It was quite likely she would.

Her cheerful grin, however, banished my doubts.

'Want to see something, Linda?' she asked, and fished up a thin gold chain from under her uniform. At the end of it was a ring with a fine large ruby and two pearls.

'You're engaged?' I asked.

She looked alarmed. 'Not exactly. Not yet. At least, Gordon doesn't want it announced yet. That's why I'm wearing it like this. Don't say anything to anyone, will you?'

'What does "anyone" mean?'

'Everyone.'

'Even your family?'

'Well, you won't be seeing them, will you?' she said, rather awkwardly, I thought.

'Why did you say that, Frances? I know I haven't seen David for some time, but he's away, isn't he?'

'No,' she said, unwillingly. 'He didn't take that newspaper job after all.'

I saw down slowly on my bed. I had just come off night duty and I was really too tired to argue. Frances, on the other hand, had her day off, and time to kill. She was loafing around before going home.

'Am I supposed to know what all this is about?' I asked, smiling.

'That Torringfield man is in a private ward, you know,' she said, not looking at me. 'He let me in the other night.'

'So he told me,' I replied, grimly. 'I hope you realised what kept me from being there in time.'

'I heard,' she said, without much interest. 'He's ... nice, isn't he?'

'It's a matter of opinion,' I said, crisply. 'I suppose, you told David about him?'

'Naturally,' she said, flinging up her little round chin, her eyes filled with sudden anger. 'Our David's silly enough over you. I like you as a friend, but I'm not sure that–'

'That you want me as a sister? I shouldn't worry, if I were you,' I retorted.

'I didn't mean that,' she said, her anger falling away quickly, as it always did, leaving her looking rather like a child who has just come out of a kicking tantrum and is sorry and ashamed. 'What I meant was, well, we don't know much about you, and what we do know – well, I don't want our David hurt any more than he is.'

'Supposing I run into any of your family.

44

Am I to act as if I'd never heard of Gordon Evans?'

She nodded.

'You didn't have to show me that thing or even mention it,' I mused. 'Why did you?'

Her face crumpled suddenly, and I had a horrible fear that she was going to break down. She put her forefingers up to the corners of her mouth, and managed to stop her lips from wobbling; an idiotic childish gesture she had never lost.

'It's all right, Linda. I'm not going to howl. I know you hate people bawling,' she said, trying to laugh. 'I showed you because, well – oh, heavens, do we have to be like this? There isn't anyone else I'd rather tell. There isn't anyone else I'd rather have for a sister if our David's got to marry someone, except that–'

I felt infinitely weary. Sister Tutor had always told us to keep our lives free from emotions and anxieties, because they sapped our strength beyond all else. Up till these last few weeks I had managed to take her advice. I had managed to put the past behind me, but now I couldn't. It had caught up with me. The past, and the entanglement of David. I just wanted to crawl between the sheets and sleep and sleep, and be swamped by forgetfulness. But I knew that was now impossible. If I slept at all, I would be dream-haunted. Alan ... David ... Frances and her Gordon...

I went over to her and sat beside her on the bed. Acutely embarrassed at this demonstration of female affection, I slipped an arm round her and held her in a firm grip.

'Silly mug,' I said, huskily. 'If it's any comfort to you, I won't marry David. Ever. Here, I'll tell you something. He's already asked me, and I said no.'

I was terribly afraid she'd start hugging me. The whole of David's family were the type who threw arms round each other and hugged on the slightest excuse. I loved the warmth, the affectionate atmosphere of that family, but the public demonstration of it made me curl up inside.

Frances knew better than to do anything so foolhardy. She turned round, however, in a great deal of surprise, and said, 'Honestly?' and then her pleasure fled. 'But David – he loves you so much, Linda. Was it that night, the last time you saw him?'

I nodded, and she waited.

'Frances, I'd tell you a lot more. I'd tell you everything if I could be certain that you wouldn't blurt it all out,' I said, desperately.

She nodded. 'I know. That's me all over. But just tell me one thing. That Torringfield man. Everyone's crazy about him. You know, he's got that beastly sort of charm. But he's rotten, underneath, isn't he? And you're not … you're not mixed up with him, are you?'

'What makes you think I might be?' I fenced, wondering how on earth I could get out of this without giving her the wrong impression.

'Well, you do seem to be all hot and bothered about him. Oh, I know you haven't *said* anything – you never did *say* anything – but you haven't been the same since he's been here. And him coming back into hospital again. Oh, I can't put it into words, but I just *feel* that he's at the bottom of everything.'

'Did you ever read the newspaper accounts of that case, two years ago?' I murmured.

'A bit. I don't remember much about it. It was the others talking about it that reminded me,' she confessed.

'Well, he was supposed to be mixed up in something, and then the people who started the case called it off. Remember?'

She agreed, reluctantly. She was doubtful about it all.

'Well, it doesn't follow then that he was guilty, does it? People don't call off law cases they start for nothing, do they?'

'There's no smoke without fire,' she said, stolidly.

'Yes, you've heard someone else say that,' I told her. 'Well, rightly or wrongly, he got in the newspapers. If you were distantly related to him, would you refuse to speak to him

47

because of that?'

'Are you *related* to him?' she exclaimed.

'He's distantly related by marriage to my family,' I said carefully.

'Then you *have* got a family!'

'Everyone's got a family,' I said, getting up off her bed, and feeling irritable that I had given in to a whim and told her as much as I had. 'They don't necessarily have much to do with them, or talk about them, for that matter.'

'You're so funny,' she complained. 'Everyone else talks about their people. Everyone else gets homesick. You don't seem to be made the same way as us.' And then she flushed and looked genuinely sorry, and I realised that I was letting my face give too much away. 'Gosh, I'm sorry, Linda – I never realised you might be feeling awful and homesick underneath and not letting anyone know. Gosh, I'm sorry!'

'Oh, shut up, shut up! Get out, can't you, and let me get some sleep,' I yelled.

I began tearing my clothes off, and she took the hint and put on her outdoor clothes and went. She hesitated at the door and I thought she was going to come back and do something silly, but she didn't. She finally went, and I locked the door behind her.

In my pyjamas at last, I crept into bed. I was shivering. I buried my face in the pillow

48

and dug my nails into the palms of my hands, and lay stiff and taut, struggling against the storm of tears that threatened to engulf me. After the struggle, I felt spent. If I gave way now, I knew I would never be able to go through with my training. I had steeled myself to go through with it all by a simple and perhaps not very wise move. I made myself see the patients as occupied beds, each with a number and a complaint. I never ever thought about them after I left the wards.

In my present low state, I suddenly saw them as people. Perhaps it was because I had just been put on the women's surgical ward. There was old Granny Greygates, who looked at me with shrewd, kindly eyes, and did her best to draw me out, as she called it. It was exhausting work, smiling and fencing with her, while I blanket-bathed her and made her bed. But she was so like my old nannie that there were times when I dared not look at her face at all. She had an inoperable growth. She wouldn't ever leave the hospital. I don't know whether she knew that. She had a serene smile always, although her face was a ghastly colour, and drawn with pain.

There was young Mary Abbotts, who had been beautiful but was now a travesty of a human, with half her face and neck missing. She had been on a picnic with her boyfriend, and the stove had exploded, and she had got the worst of it. In time, a long, long time, she would be able to raise her face from her neck, and plastic surgery might make her less hideous. It was not pain, nor the repeated trips to the operation theatre, nor the fact that she had lost beauty and youth, nor even that she had lost her boyfriend that bothered her. She had been in hospital so long, and was so very homesick.

And then there was young Judy Niel, a young married woman, who had had her ovaries removed, and cried into the night because she couldn't have any children. There was Maude Wellan, who had had an important administrative job, and now had nothing but a future of sitting about, going carefully, never being really well, after losing a kidney.

Fourteen beds in that ward, with women whose faces, whose eyes, wrung the heart. I tossed and turned, and heard Sister Tutor's warning voice.

'Don't ever care personally about them, since it limits one's powers of helping them.'

'Don't ever care ... don't ever care...' thudded in my brain and I saw Mother lying dying in the big four-poster at home, begging my father to call off the case against Alan Torringfield. 'Don't ever care ... don't ever care ... don't ever care...' Doctor Farnham saying severely to me, 'If I had had my

50

hands free, and no anxiety weakening her, I could have saved her. As it is–' and he had raised expressive hands. My father looking at me, that last time I saw him, with hatred in his eyes.

I got to sleep at last, but I awakened early, with a furious headache. It was raining again. September was drawing to a sullen close. I would have given a lot at that moment to be away from the hospital for a stretch of hours, to forget everyone I knew, go away from it all, especially from the smell of antiseptic. I think it was Alan, perhaps, reminding me of that night long ago, when I had worn that lovely gown, and smelt of a new and haunting perfume I had just tried out. Where my world was gracious and beautiful, and everybody one saw was *whole*.

I went on to the wards in a miserable frame of mind, and I think my mood reflected itself on to my patients. They seemed fretful, even the habitually cheerful ones, and the other nurses who made up the night staff were not in their best moods, either. I dropped a clinical thermometer, and broke some glasses washing up. My fellow junior was guilty of breaking a hypodermic needle, and for our sins we called down the wrath of Night Sister on our heads.

I thought the morning would never come, but when it did, and I finally went off duty, I had a shattering surprise. Someone said, as I collected by way of personal mail, a familiar pale grey envelope, square and heavy, 'Last day of September. What a day to be born on!'

I ripped open the square flap with shaking hands, and realised as I did so, why it had come.

It was from Aunt Berenice. 'Darling Linda,' she wrote. 'Many happy returns of your birthday.'

Chapter Four

She had included a generous cheque, because as she said, she didn't know what my tastes were these days, and she had included also an invitation to spend my next leave there. That was the most important part.

I went out into another day of heavy rain with a lightened heart. I had a stretch of hours off duty, and instead of spending them pouring over text-books, I decided to get some much-needed fresh air. Alan Torringfield was still safely in the hospital, and I walked out of Bardmore's that day feeling very much like a prisoner emerging from his gaol.

I just walked. I don't know how long I had been walking, before I decided to have a coffee, and slipped into a tea-shop. It was good coffee, milky and hot, and I sat in a corner sipping it gratefully. The tea-shop smelt of cooking. Warm and humid, with steamed-up windows, and there were only a few people in the shop. I relaxed and decided not to think any more about the hospital, but about that precious week's leave. Aunt Berenice's cheque would be helpful for some decent clothes. I must look well-groomed if I were to take her invitation seriously. One didn't dress anyhow at Marleigh Park. What was more, my father wouldn't be there. Aunt Berenice had stressed that point. He had a new directorship which would take him to the States for some part of every year, and she wanted to see me at those times. I wished he had got his beastly new job before this. I had only another year to spend at Bardmore's, and then I had intended to try and get a job abroad, if I qualified. Once I'd got my S.R.N I'd be free. My heart always soared as I thought about it. Where would I go? Australia or the Near East? Africa, perhaps. Anywhere where I need never fear Alan, or anyone else. But now I wasn't so sure, with this new chance of going home. That rather altered things.

Someone touched me on the shoulder, and I knocked my cup over in surprise. Although I knew Alan was still in the hospital, I think I must have expected to find him beside me, having got out on some outrageous pretext. I believe his name sprang to my lips. I know I said something, and then I saw it was David.

David with a face ravaged with some emotion I couldn't define before it changed to laughing embarrassment at the mess of coffee all over the table. A waitress came and mopped it up, and he ordered more, for both of us. More coffee, which neither of us drank.

'Linda,' he said huskily. 'I followed you, from Bardmore's, and I hadn't the nerve to speak to you. Till you came in here.'

'You followed me?' I repeated stupidly.

He nodded. 'I went to the hospital, half meaning to send you up a note. Frances said you might be off duty today.'

'What did you want me for, David?'

He looked blank. 'What did I want you for?'

'I mean, anything special?' I laughed helplessly. 'David, you left me with your nose in the air, and frost all over you. I never thought you'd want to see me again.'

He fiddled with his spoon, and lit the eternal cigarette with what was, for him, a nervous gesture.

'I know. I've been in hell since then. I meant not to see you any more. I've gone through back newspaper files, and tortured myself over that old case. God, I wish it hadn't happened, Linda, that wretched law case that fizzled out. Why did it have to happen?' And without waiting for me to attempt to answer that, he rushed on: 'It isn't any use. It didn't matter what had happened, doesn't matter what will happen, it all adds up to the same. I can't do without you, Linda.'

We stared miserably at each other. I had

said to him that if he went away, I couldn't bear it, and yet in point of fact I had been able to bear it. I hadn't found myself longing to see him to pour out my troubles, and that surely was the crucial test? Rather, I had been glad that I hadn't been seeing him, so that I didn't fall into the trap again of telling him things I'd rather keep hidden.

The question I had been dreading, suddenly voiced itself.

'Have you missed me, Linda?'

Time seemed to stand still. I saw, in that second, things that really mattered, and those that didn't, all in their right perspective. It doesn't often happen like that. I usually managed to see things the way I wanted to see them, but in that moment, everything was crystal clear. I saw the faces of the women in the surgical ward, and I saw Alan and myself, David and Frances in their individual unhappiness and mental confusion, and I saw Aunt Berenice, inviting me back home in my father's absence. I felt sick at the pit of my stomach, and I said something I wouldn't have said at any other time, and I knew what it would lead to. Knowing that, I went on, and I knew all the other things I was going to say. Once in a lifetime one can throw everything to the winds, and tell the truth, and that was what happened to me just then, in a small café with cooling coffee in front of me, and

David with his heart in his eyes.

'No, I haven't, David. I hardly ever thought about you.'

I couldn't go on looking at him, and watching his hurt.

'Take it, David. Take it, my dear. I can't help what my heart does, and I'm not going to mislead you.'

'Linda!' he whispered.

'David, about Alan Torringfield,' I went on, remorselessly. 'Did Frances tell you she got something out of me about him? That he's distantly related to me? Very distantly, by marriage, anyway.'

He shook his head. I don't think he was really listening.

'You've *got* to listen,' I told him. 'I'm as confused and miserable as you are. I've got my own troubles, as you have. But I'm going to tell you, David. You always wanted to know. I'm going to tell you.'

I waited for the effect, but he still seemed stunned.

'He's in hospital now. In a private ward.'

'I know,' David said. 'Frances told me that.'

'He'll be coming out soon. I can't imagine that even he will be able to stand up to the diet and tests for a gastric stomach he hasn't got.'

'What about him, Linda?'

'He's making me promise to go back –

well, as we were – or else he'll see that Matron knows about that old business. And that means I'll be kicked out of Bardmore's.'

His face flamed with anger. 'The swine. Let me meet him, Linda. I'll settle him.'

'You haven't asked me what I mean by ... as we were.'

'Oh, well, you said, didn't you. Distant cousins.' He looked into my eyes, and couldn't help checking up on that. 'You were just that, weren't you?'

I shook my head. 'I thought I was in love with him, once.'

He took that, and I watched his white face with a feeling that I was slowly killing him.

'Engaged, were you?'

I laughed bitterly. 'No, Alan doesn't get engaged to anyone. He just let me down when I needed him. You've read the newspaper files. So you'll be able to see how he let me down. Now he sees I don't want him anymore, he's going to alter all that.'

'And you're going to let him?'

'David, I told you – the only thing I want in the world is to get my S.R.N.'

'But heavens, Linda, wouldn't it be simpler to go to Matron and explain?' David burst out.

I considered the point, gravely, so that I shouldn't go into peals of hysterical laughter. 'Have you ever met Matron?' I ventured at last.

'Well, no, but Frances has painted what I should consider a fair picture of her for us,' he admitted, with a shadow of a smile.

'I can't honestly see Matron saying, "Well, send the bounder to me and I'll fix him." I can't honestly see Matron saying, "Well done, Nurse Fane, for being loyal to the hospital; in spite of being mixed up in court proceedings a little matter of two years ago, we need you here at Bardmore's." Can you, David?'

He saw my point.

'What are you going to do, then?'

'David, I'm going back to Alan. What can I lose?'

'But you don't love him!' he exclaimed, reddening again.

I had the grace to flush myself, as I recalled how Alan had kissed me. I spread appealing hands, begging him to understand without asking for words. 'I don't *love* him, but he – I–'

I floundered. I couldn't go on. I just hated the whole wretched business. Those threatening tears came to the surface this time, and I angrily rubbed the back of my hand up my cheek.

'It's my birthday today,' I said, for no reason at all.

David got up, noisily scraping back his chair. 'Let's get out of here,' he said.

We walked down to the river. There is a

savage loveliness about the Thames on a wet autumn day. The flaming yellow and crimson of the leaves set against a grey background; the grey of river, buildings, parapet and pavements, all rain-washed and gleaming with reflections. We stood staring at it for a time, saying nothing. We were very close together, and there was comfort in David being near to me. I asked myself why I couldn't be in love with him. He was so safe, so dependable, so... I looked up quickly at him. Surely the hunger in his eyes should set light to a spark in me? He suddenly caught me to him, and his lips found mine. In all that rain-washed stretch of embankment, we were alone with our misery and our emotion.

'Linda, Linda, I don't care for this Torringfield, I don't care for the hospital, or what's gone by in your life. I only know I want you, Linda, I'll make you love me. They say love begets love. I'll *make* you love me!'

The desperation in his voice caught at me, and I was crying with an abandon that terrified me. I don't remember ever crying like that before. Even when Mother died. At that time I froze up and covered up the lump that was my throat. Now it all came out, and I was lost before the torrent. David held me, crooning soft little endearments that I missed, beneath the noise of my own crying. When it was over, I was so spent that I leaned exhausted against him, and let him make plans, absurd ambitious plans, which I knew could never come to anything. I let him say just what he liked, and I hadn't the heart to mention to him then that I was making up my mind to go home for my week's leave. That could come later.

I felt better for that emotional storm, however. Tired, but washed free of everything that bothered me, I left David at last and went back to the wards, having set in water in my room the huge bunch of dahlias David had bought me from the flower-stall outside the hospital. The problem of how I was to go home without incurring Alan's unwelcome company, I shelved for the moment. I knew within the next forty-eight hours that he was out of hospital, but until I heard from him, I imagined I had nothing to fear.

Towards the end of that week, I managed to get a late night pass on the same evening as Frances. I had been shopping and bought some new clothes for my week, and I let her see them.

Whether it was wise or not, I didn't stop to think. But Frances had new clothes herself, bought by her father. So it didn't matter so much. She wasn't inquisitive enough to ask the reason for mine, because her head was full of her own new things, bought for

61

Gordon's benefit, and by the time she realised I had a week off, I hoped I would be on my journey, leaving a note behind for her. Frances had no eyes or ears for anything at the moment but Gordon Evans.

I had seen him on the wards that morning. He was such a good houseman that I couldn't bring myself to loathe him as much as I felt I ought. But the way his fair hair was brushed into impeccable waves, and the very brightness of his keen blue eyes, were major affronts, I felt. He was really much too good-looking for a surgeon.

'Do you like this red topcoat, Linda?' Frances asked, having inspected my wardrobe of soft blues and grey. 'Will it suit me, d'you suppose?'

She looked utterly lovely in it. There was a small red hat to go with it, that sat wickedly on the top of her black hair and made her look like something on the front of a glossy magazine, rather than a Bardmore's nurse. I said so, and she seemed to like that. 'That's what Gordon says,' she said, flushing.

'Frances, how involved are you?' I asked nervously.

'It's all the way,' she said simply. 'I love Gordon, and I don't care if–'

'Don't care *what?*' I asked, leaning forward.

'He loves me, too, I know he does,' she muttered, feverishly. 'Linda, you'll keep your promise about tonight? You won't back out – about coming home, I mean?'

I hesitated. We had arranged to keep this evening in an odd sort of way. I was to go to dinner and a show with David, Frances was presumably dining out with Gordon Evans, and then she was to meet David and me, and go back home together, the three of us, for supper.

'What will David say? Won't he want to know who you've been spending the evening with?' I protested.

'I told him some fellow from the hospital who'd got to be back on duty, and I asked him not to mention it at home, because Mother will jump to conclusions, you know how she does, and anyway, nothing's settled.'

'You let David think it's just a casual date?'

'You let David think there wasn't anyone else in your life, didn't you?' she accused.

'At first, but he knows now,' I said, quietly.

Her eyes opened wide. 'You told him? About that man Torringfield?'

'Never mind what I've told him. I've told him a lot of things because David's got sense and won't let a word out. You can't say the same for you, so shut up. And don't start trying to get anything out of David to satisfy that frightful curiosity of yours,' I finished.

'I won't – if you won't breathe a word to anyone about Gordon,' she bargained.

'Silly, isn't it, all this secrecy. I sometimes wonder why we don't come out into the open and be damned to everything,' I muttered. 'Frances, why don't you? You know why I don't. It isn't in me to talk about my private affairs. Besides, the only thing that matters to me is nursing, and I must get my S.R.N. But it isn't that with you. Why don't you tell everyone about Gordon – your people, I mean, even if you don't tell anyone here?'

She hesitated. 'If I were sure that Gordon cared for me, I would,' she admitted painfully. 'But I'm not sure.'

I felt a brute. I knew what twisting the knife meant. As I stared at her, she let her hand wander to the place where that ring of his lay, behind her uniform. 'It doesn't mean a thing,' she muttered, bitterly. 'Not to him. But I don't care. I love him, and I'm going to snatch every minute with him while I can.'

I watched her compassionately. The question must have been in my face, though I couldn't ask it outright. I hadn't got the heart to.

'And when it's over,' she whispered, biting fiercely on her bottom lip, 'I'm getting the hell out of here. If you think I'm crazy about bedpans and vomiting patients, you're wrong. I hate it. Hate it!'

'You mean that,' I said, amazed. 'Then

what made you take it up in the first place?'

'Why did you?' she retorted.

'It was something that happened to me. Never mind what. But I made up my mind to do something to help all the sick people. It isn't as romantic as it sounds, either,' I said hastily. 'Call it conscience, if you like, or remorse. Never mind. I wanted to do it. I still want it. I'll always want it. There isn't anything else. I might revolt sometimes, but I'll always come back to it. I think it's in me.'

'I believe you're right,' she marvelled. 'Christmas, I wish someone had said that to me at first! I'd have been too scared to start if I'd seen how it got people. Linda, I just joined for – well, something to do. I knew girls who'd become nurses, and they seemed happy enough, and it seemed fun, the way they went on. They never told how beastly it was, behind it all. They looked nice in uniform and they looked responsible bending over the beds. I never knew they had to hold down struggling patients. I'd never seen a haemorrhage or a patient just back from the op. theatre. I'd no idea about performing Last Offices, and Linda, the sight of a body on the mortuary trolley still makes me want to throw up my last meal.'

I studied her worriedly. She was still muddling through her written work, while I seemed to lap it up. I never had difficulty in remembering names of diseases or drugs,

65

and I could reel off the names of the instruments in the op. theatre without turning a hair, but just those things were insurmountable obstacles to Frances. She still boggled at using the stomach pump, and catheter tests were agony for the patient no less than herself. No, she wasn't a nurse.

'You should have said all this before,' I said, quietly. 'Why don't you get out now? It can't be good for you, and you'll never get anywhere if you feel like that about it.'

'I can't. I'll never see Gordon again if I do,' she said.

Chapter Five

The evening with David was marred from the first by a note from Alan, now out of hospital. It was addressed from a mews flat in the West End. I could imagine the sort of place. He would have picked it up from the friend of a friend. The owner of the lease would be as unknown to him as the man in the moon. There would be the usual truckle bed, made up divan fashion with hectic cushions; the same preponderance of books on shelves and gramophone records all over the place. There would be a gas-ring, or small old-fashioned cooker in the corner, delicately hidden by a Chinese screen, and the whole place would be approached by a pair of rickety wooden steps up to an equally rickety wooden balcony.

I knew it as if I had already seen it. Alan specialised in them. He had never paid a farthing for rent in all his adult life. He never intended to. He cadged as he went; food, lodging, even fares. He once travelled half way round the world at someone else's expense, simply because he was an amusing companion, and his ability to cadge wine had to be seen to be believed.

His note said that I was to spend my next time off with him. I was to telephone him to say when it was. I counted the hours to my week's leave, and wondered if I could find someone to swap with me, so that I could go off the next morning.

David looked very nice. He looked at my new steel-blue silk dress with approval. 'That colour suits you,' he said, and there was the old faint wonderment in his voice, as if he couldn't believe his good luck in having a girl like me to take out. It made me feel wicked, and very wretched. I ought to be on tiptoe with excitement at having a stretch of hours to spend with him, instead of which I was feverishly pushing the hours by me, until I could board a train for Marleigh Park.

I don't remember the show, or what we ate for dinner. I only remember his choosing an exceptionally good wine. It tasted like velvet. I said so, and he laughed in a pleased way.

'I like a girl to appreciate good wine,' he said. 'They nearly all want cocktails or gin.'

'How do you know, David?' I asked, and because teasing from me was so rare, he took it as a step forward, and I was sorry.

'Oh, Linda, I don't care what you say you feel about me. I'm only so very glad, so very grateful, that I can still see you sometimes. I feel, deep inside me, that some day you'll

68

feel the same way as I do. Or at least, that you'll feel safe enough in my keeping to trust your life to me.'

'David, please. Not tonight.'

'Why not? Why not tonight? Linda, I suppose you wouldn't, you couldn't consider–'

'No, David,' I said, quickly. Too quickly.

'You don't know what I was going to say.'

'I think I do. I'm afraid I do. Perhaps I'm presuming, but it's just that I don't want you to say anything that'd make me answer you in a way that would hurt you. I've hurt you enough. David, for what it's worth, I can't bear to hurt you, but don't get excited about it. Remember the poet who said something about "Tread softly, you're treading on my heart?" I can't remember exactly how it goes, but you make me feel that you're thinking that. The way you look at me.'

'It would be true,' he said, soberly.

'David, I can't bear it. Tonight,' I said, desperately, 'just before I came out, I got a note from Alan Torringfield.'

His face darkened, and he waited.

'He wants me to spend my next free time with him. He didn't know I was getting time off tonight.'

'What are you going to do about it?'

I didn't answer him directly. Instead, I said, 'I'm going home for a week.'

If I had said I was going to the moon for a

week, I don't think he would have looked more stunned.

'Home?' he whispered.

I nodded. 'Home. To Marleigh Park. My aunt invited me. I want to go home, and yet I don't. I shall go. I'm hoping I'll be able to sort myself out, once I'm back there.'

The writer in him wanted a picture of it. 'What will it be like, Linda?'

'I haven't got a snap of the place with me,' I confessed, ruefully. 'Oh, but you'll have seen it, in the newspapers.'

That was unfortunate, that reference to the case. We both flushed, and there was an awkward moment.

I rushed on, frantically trying not to spoil the evening: It's red brick, and sprawling, and covered in creepers, and hosts of windows, and little lawns dropping from terraces, and you go through a stretch of woodland to it, and there are game-keepers and still quite a few gardeners and–'

He was watching me critically.

'David, it means – I'm sorry, but I might as well tell you – it means silk sheets and being waited on hand and foot, even in these days. It means quiet voices and visitors who are important and interesting. It means belonging and that means so very much to me, especially now. And it means smells ... how can I put it? No more ether and carbolic, only old wood and leather, the pungent smell of bonfires outside, and my aunt's special perfume...'

My voice broke and I couldn't go on.

David said, speculatively, 'I'd like to see you against that background, Linda. But then I'd also like to see you in hospital, doing all the things which our Frances describes with such revolting detail. I can't imagine you in either place. Is that very strange?'

'If you think of me in your odd moments, how do you think of me?' I asked, recklessly, and with rare curiosity.

'*If* I think of you!' he exclaimed. '*How* I think of you? Standing in the kitchen of the small house I dream of, making a meal for me,' he began, but I cut him short.

'David, no! I didn't mean that. What I meant was, if you can't think of me as a nurse, when I've been only that since you first met me, then surely, surely it means that I've failed?'

I could hear the anxiety in my own voice, and he looked up sharply.

'What are you going to do, Linda, after a week in this grand home of yours, if you find you can't bear the hospital?'

'That's what I can't bear to think about,' I whispered.

And so the evening fled by, with just that sort of intimate conversation. David always trying to steer the conversation back to what he wanted for us both, my trying to keep it

71

in more businesslike channels. I forgot to talk to him about Frances, and happily there was no more opportunity for Alan to creep back into the conversation.

When I left David, I felt wretched again. The last vestige of fun was swept away for me, by his farewell. Frances tactfully prolonged her farewells to her family, while David and I walked slowly up the road. By the time she joined us, I was too miserable to care if I went to Bardmore's with or without her.

'Will you think of me during that week, Linda?'

'Of course, David.'

'Enough to telephone me, perhaps?'

I hesitated, and he noticed, and again there was that stricken look in his eyes.

'David, if I telephone you, my aunt will know about it, and she'll jump to conclusions. You know I want to be fair, don't you? I don't want anyone to get the wrong slant on us, until – if – well, you know what I'm trying to say.'

He nodded, his mouth turning down at the corners. I had had a trying time at supper, going back to his family after so long a time. They were such nice people, and yet tonight they had seemed unreal to me. Perhaps it was because, in my mind, I was already making that journey down to Marleigh.

'David, don't kiss me goodbye. Wait till I come back from Marleigh. I feel, I really feel I shall know better then, how you stand. Help me, David. Help me to ... not hurt you any more than I have to.'

Again I was conscious of not having said the thing he wanted, any more than I had said quite the thing that I had tried to. Clumsy, awkward, hurting him by that, anyway.

He did kiss me, nevertheless. Hungrily, as if he couldn't bear to let me go without kissing me. We stood behind a pillar-box, I recall, so that if Frances came rushing down the street, she wouldn't see us embracing.

'Linda, I don't know how I've managed all these weeks without you. I tried, heaven knows, but it wouldn't work. Linda, don't let them push me out of your thoughts. Let me stay, my dear, let me stay.'

And then, with infinite relief, I heard his sister's running footsteps, and I didn't have to answer.

I got away to Marleigh two days later. On the train I churned over my mixed impressions. I hadn't had another communication from Alan, and I hadn't telephoned him. There just hadn't been time. Granny Greygates had been extra sweet to me, and told me, with a depressing conviction, that she wouldn't be there when I came back. Frances was treading the heights because Gordon

Evans had smiled openly at her across a patient's bed, with Sister Winston standing by, and all the other student nurses were wildly excited because of the advent of a new honorary surgeon, who was reputed to be not only good-looking and extremely wealthy, but a bachelor.

Frances had said to me, in the privacy of our shared room, pretty much what David had said two nights ago. 'What will it be like, your home?'

I didn't think she had heard me say I was going there, at first. She had been staring absently out of the window, down at the yard where the bath chairs outside the out-patients' department stood in a depressing row, and the heaps of coal and coke occupied the yard's corners. Always, when she was absent-minded these days, she twirled at her ring beneath her uniform, and my heart would go into my mouth in case someone noticed her.

'I daren't think,' I said. 'I haven't been there for two years.'

'Are there servants?'

'There were,' I said, carefully.

'Dogs and horses? Cars? Parties?'

She looked round as I didn't answer. I was asking myself that same question. Parties had gone on, despite Mother's illness. That had been her wish. But now? With no young people in the place?

74

'All but the parties,' I said, slowly. 'Bridge, of course, and dreary company directors' after-dinner conversation, and their dreadful wives. Very dull.'

She looked disappointed, but satisfied. I wondered why she had asked. Frances loved the gay life, but she didn't begrudge anyone else the things she hadn't.

She came over to me suddenly, and said quickly, 'I'm going to hug you, whether you like it or not. And I hope you have a perfectly wonderful time, and find yourself a marvellous piece of male, for I'm scared about a super person like you getting tied up with that Torringfield man.'

I tore away from her quickly. It was one thing to howl all over her brother's shoulder, but quite a different thing to let Frances see me go to pieces. I wondered afterwards if she thought she had offended me. I thought about it for quite a bit on the train, for there hadn't been an opportunity of finding out. I didn't see her again after that.

Pope came to the station in the green limousine to meet me, a sure sign that my father wasn't at home. That was his car, and holy. The sight of it, and Pope in his immaculate green livery at the wheel, struck me like a blow. Two years of catching London buses had made me feel strange about stepping into the back of a private car, and not having to close the door. The

75

station master was new, but the ticket-collector was our old one and recognised me. He looked curious, but on the whole pleased to see me. Pope was so inscrutable that I couldn't tell if he were pleased or disapproving.

I had kept thinking about Marleigh all the way in the train, between Frances and the rest of the hospital memories. I had kept harking back to it, trying to make myself picture it over and over again, so that I wouldn't be upset at the sight of it. But I might have saved myself the trouble. I was so upset that I could only nod in a distant sort of way to Chalfont, who opened the door, and his effusive and obviously very real welcome almost tripped me up and tore down my last shred of command. He looked much older than two years seemed to warrant, but still, what could you expect a butler to be like, with twenty-four months of unrelieved taking the brunt of my father's ill-humour?

The sight of Aunt Berenice, however, finished me. I had to have some tea after that, and my face was a sight.

She was a lovely person. Never surprised at anything, and deeply tolerant of everything and everyone, even my father.

'There, there, my dear,' she comforted, stroking my hair. 'It's the strain of it all, and that ghastly hospital. I've often said to my brother, do you ever think what she's going through in that tiresome medical life, to say nothing of all the tension and anxiety of the dreadful things which happened before?'

'But of course, he doesn't think,' I choked, making a feeble and entirely unsuccessful attempt at a joke.

'Try not to make your face look too unsightly, darling. I've someone I want you to meet,' she said, quietly, knowing that the advent of a visitor was the one thing to jerk me back to my senses.

I drank tea and we soberly talked things out of our systems. She didn't mention my mother, but she did touch on the subject of Alan. She knew he was back in this country. He had already asked her for money, and when he had found that my father was in America, he had impudently asked to be invited down to the Park.

'He was in our hospital,' I said, and told her what had happened.

She looked straight at me. I always had marvelled at that serene face of hers, which suggested to me that she found the world such a good place, and people at their very worst merely tiresome.

'Aunt Berenice, don't ask me if I'm going to see him. I don't know. It was such a struggle to get into Bardmore's as things were – I don't think I could bear to be kicked out of there now.'

'Does it mean so much to you, dear?'

I looked round the room. It was large and gracious. Ivory and lilac, with an Adam fireplace, a fine old ceiling, and a few choice water-colours that must have been worth a fortune. A few rare pieces of Eastern carving, cabinets and tables, and tall windows giving out on to the choicest view of the park. Fine old china and silver, hand-embroidered napkins, paper-thin sandwiches, and the delicate aroma of Aunt Berenice's special blend of tea, contrasted sadly with the nostalgic memory of hospital thick white china and doorstep bread. Most ungratefully I had a rush of homesickness for the hospital, and it was much more potent than I had felt for Marleigh Park. Had I outgrown this old life?

I spread out hands which had become roughened with cleaning sluices with abrasive powder, and nails cut short for convenience, which had not seen a manicurist for two years, and said softly, 'I'm afraid it does, Aunt Berenice.' And I felt suddenly happy for no good reason.

'I thought it might,' she said mildly, and she sounded happy, too. 'Now I want you to meet Nigel. We had tea early, and I sent him down to the stables to see the new cocker litter. He's very fond of spaniels.'

'Nigel? Who is he?' I asked, anxiously surveying my face in the glass.

'I just want you to meet him as "Nigel",
one of my very special protégés,' she said,
with a smile, and I smiled, too. How often
she had done this to me in the past. Bringing a desirable male, with a Christian name
only, into the wild orbit of my men friends,
and hoping that her gentle insinuating of
the unsuspecting victim into my life would
make my unruly heart flutter in the way she
approved, and not in my way, which was all
wild torment.

We ran him to earth in the library, with
two rather new-looking spaniel puppies in
the crook of his arm. He looked up rather
guiltily, I thought, and smiled. The warmest,
most heart-stirring male smile I have ever
seen. He got hastily to his feet, and I had to
look up at him, he was so tall. He bent his
head a little, as if used to smallish women,
and I liked that trick, too.

Aunt Berenice murmured, 'Nigel, not
here, dear. Stephens won't like that a bit,'
and she stared thoughtfully at the offending
puppies. 'This is my only niece, Linda.
Nigel, I fear, has a trick of breaking rules in
the most innocent way, but he breaks them,
nevertheless.'

I found myself going pink as she smiled at
me.

'Rather like you, Linda dear,' she murmured, and left us.

How can I describe that week at Marleigh

Park? Nigel appeared to be staying in the house, the only guest at the time. Although I suspected Aunt Berenice of matchmaking, I could no more have resisted the tug of his personality than I could have resisted the tug of the current when swimming against the tide.

We rode together at dawn, through golden-brown woodland. We drove about in the Daimler, and in the slick black car which Nigel had apparently come down in. We talked, mainly about the things we liked. We went dancing, we inspected every inch of the estate, but spent most of our time in the stables. He loved dogs with a passion that might have matched my own, in those far-off days. Dogs were a thing I had missed, this last two years.

And yet I didn't mention the hospital to him. I don't know why. It was as if I were fighting to keep him in the picture of my home, and not to let him intrude into the new life I had been striving to keep separate. He was to be, my heart clamoured, just an episode, and I wouldn't let myself think of what it would be like when I went back to London, and thrust him out of my mind, and took up the old tangle of Alan and David.

Nigel had a camera, and took pictures of me, and I took some of him. I caught that haunting sweet smile of his, and the tenderness of his mouth in some way reminded me of David. But Nigel had a strength behind that tenderness, and there was no dream quality about him. I knew that he wasn't a writer or artist, although his knowledge of fine art kept Aunt Berenice on her toes, and she reckoned herself a connoisseur.

'Do you like my Nigel, Linda, dear?' Aunt Berenice asked me, the last evening I was there.

At her suggestion I wore my new white dress, and she lent me her pearl pendant and ear-rings.

'He's all right,' I murmured.

'You're very beautiful, my dear. I want ... I would so much like...'

'No!' I cried, and was bewildered to find a pain at my heart. Just as if someone had stuck a knife in me. 'Don't matchmake, Aunt Berenice. He's gentry, and you know what I am. My father said so. And it's true. Let me go back to my slum and don't let him know about it.'

I had hurt her, but I couldn't help it.

'Oh, but I've told him that you're a nurse in hospital, dear. He was extremely interested. It seems he didn't know it.'

'Why did you tell him that? I didn't want him to know! I wanted to ... I wanted to keep him part of this pleasant week. I didn't want him to ... to come into my other life at all.'

'One can't relegate people to places or sections of our lives, my dear,' she said mildly. 'You might remember that, in connection with Alan.'

That was all she said, but during dinner she observed, 'Linda hasn't told you she has a passion for medicine, then, Nigel. I suppose that means, my dear, that you have kept a similar secret of your love of the scalpel.'

There was a tiny smile lurking round Aunt Berenice's mouth which in anyone else could well have been called malicious. Nigel looked frankly agonised as his head shot up, and his eyes met hers.

'Oh, Miss Fane,' he said, reproachfully.

'Are you a doctor, then?' I asked, sharply.

'Silly child,' Aunt Berenice said. 'I didn't introduce you both formally, because I wanted this thing to develop naturally. But now I suppose at this late stage I'll have to make formal introduction.'

I listened dazedly, and was conscious of a violent admixture of emotions. A crushing disappointment, and the student nurse's natural embarrassment in the presence of her betters. I wanted to be up and on my feet, with my hands behind me, not sitting there at dinner with him, arguing, as we had been, friendly fashion, over the nice point of whether Turner's art was too old-fashioned to merit modern enthusiasm.

'...Nigel Armstrong,' Aunt Berenice was saying, and reeling off a list of relevant facts, from which I gathered that my newest man-friend had a private nursing home, clinics, consultant rooms in Harley Street, and was, moreover, the newest honorary at Bardmore's, the one all the student nurses were going soppy about.

Chapter Six

I suppose it would be an exaggeration to say that the evening finished without incident. There may not have been anything actually happening, nor any particular tension in the air. Aunt Berenice and Nigel Armstrong were both too well-bred to allow any such thing to be evidenced. But the happiness of the evening had gone.

I wondered, on many occasions after that, just what Aunt Berenice had hoped to do, and I can only think that she had banked on our finding out about each other during the course of conversation, somewhere during that carefree week we had spent together. Perhaps, as we hadn't had any frost in the atmosphere, she had persuaded herself that this had already happened, and that neither of us minded. I can only remind myself that she had no idea of the inner workings of life in hospital, of all the silly little points of etiquette, all the ramifications of caste down to the last six months of training. I am sure that Aunt Berenice would have thought it singularly senseless, just because of that. And so it went on, up the steps, through the huge and unwieldy staff of a hospital, and the only person who really felt comfortable and at ease in the great man's presence was Matron.

My face scorched as I recalled the things we had discussed, Nigel Armstrong and I, and the way in which we had wrangled together over the things we liked.

Aunt Berenice went further. She suggested to Nigel that he should run me up to Town the next day, and she made the fact of our being in the same hospital together seem a singularly fortunate and really rather matey occurrence. My embarrassment completely engulfed me by then, and I had nothing to say when Nigel courteously conveyed to her that nothing would give him greater pleasure than to escort me back to Town in his car. I could only get up at an impossible hour next morning, grab some sort of breakfast before Cook was about, and creep out, walking to the station because I didn't know the arrangements at present in operation about unlocking the great garages. I worked off most of my embarrassment on the train back, and also thought up some sort of story to tell Frances and her family, which wouldn't be likely to involve me too much.

Frances was a problem. I had gone home without telling her very much about it, and she would probably have had time to work up a great big hurt about the whole thing. Also she might be knee deep in trouble over

Gordon Evans by now.

The nearer I drew towards London, the further away seemed that lovely week, and all the problems and people of my life in hospital crowded back on me. I wondered if old Granny Greygates had really died, or whether, like some old folks who suffered so much, she knew she was near her end and didn't like those near her to go away for long periods. The first thing I heard on my arrival was that she had died just after I left, and that chilled me more than anything else.

There was also a letter awaiting me from Alan. I put it by, meaning to open it later when I was alone, and I found Frances looking at me rather curiously.

'Is it horribly private and personal?' she wanted to know.

We were both sitting forlornly on our beds. She had just come off duty; I had another two hours before I went on the wards. 'It's from Alan Torringfield,' I shrugged.

'Aren't you going to read it, or shall I go out of the room?' she asked, tartly.

'It can wait.'

She stared at me and I knew she was wondering what business I had in receiving letters from him, when I was so friendly with her brother.

'David knows about it,' I enlarged, cautiously.

She leaned forward.

'Linda, I'm not going to risk anything by asking questions about it. I was only going to say that if you didn't specially want to see him alone, whether you might make up a foursome. You two, Gordon and me.'

'What's the idea?' I asked, sharply.

She smiled thinly.

'Gordon and I would appreciate another couple with us sometimes, I think. He's scared that I'll want to get down to arrangements. Engagements and all that.'

'Frances, what are you playing at?' I asked, appalled by the tragedy of it all. 'If he doesn't want to get engaged, wouldn't it have a chastening effect if you left him alone for a bit? You must have a lot of other boyfriends. Heavens above, if it wouldn't do any good by not seeing him, what good do you think it will do in hanging on for ever? Surely, from the point of view of face-saving, you'd be better to start the cooling off yourself?'

Her eyes glistened and she looked quickly away. 'You would think so,' she said, in a clipped voice unlike her own. 'In fact, I know that's good sound sense. But when you're in love, you're just about insane, I sometimes think.'

I sat and stared at her, helpless, for once.

I hadn't satisfied her with my account of my week at home, I knew. Whether she guessed at the identity of the friend who was staying there, I couldn't tell. I just said that there was someone who had taken me around, and left it at that. I'm a rotten liar. But unfortunately for my story, Nigel Armstrong had passed us in the corridor as I was telling her, and he had smiled at me in the most friendly fashion. Recalling how I had slipped away from home at dawn to avoid him, I couldn't stop my face from going the colour of a beetroot, and he had raised his eyebrows in mock astonishment.

All this Frances noticed, but didn't comment upon. It would come out later, I knew very well, and I could only hope that she wouldn't embarrass me by saying it in front of other nurses.

Alan's letter had to be read at some time or other. It was pressing for an evening with him, and I thought I might just as well give it to him as not, so I told Frances I wouldn't be going home with her the next time I got off.

Aunt Berenice had asked me once, during that week at home, if I was going to mind very much about all the manual work that awaited me, after having nothing whatever to do for seven whole days. I think she believed I would find it distasteful. I had wondered, too.

Once back on the ward again, making beds, washing patients in various stages of illness, rubbing backs, making up charts, doing dressings, I was relieved to find that it wasn't a question of minding. It was all mechanical. As natural to me as eating and sleeping, almost as natural as breathing.

The only thing that really bothered me was the new patient. She was young and pretty and very ill. Her name was Elsie Gladwin, and she was Nigel's worry. No one knew what was wrong with her, and he spent a great deal more time watching her than he had need to with any of the other beds under his charge. Elsie's temperature went up and down, she lay for hours death-like, with closed eyes, and then she would be awake for long periods, fretful and very thirsty. Nigel, unobtrusive, silent of foot, seemed to be always there when she needed him.

A ripple of excitement seemed to go through the ward when he came in. He was the only honorary who was young and good-looking, and even Sister Tarling fluttered just a little when she saw him at the swing doors of the ward. I wondered what Nigel felt, with me standing behind him at a respectful distance, my hands behind my back, waiting for orders from his lips or Sister's, when not so long ago we had, in our immaculate evening dress, raised glasses to each other over my aunt's table.

If he ever felt anything at all, he gave no sign. Impartial to a marked degree, he smiled just as nicely one day at Frances when she had to pass him the blood pressure apparatus; and the junior, a child named Hilda Brigg, who was a shocking bungler though terribly well meaning, surpassed herself by being almost careful when it came to winning one of the famous Armstrong smiles.

It was something of a relief to get away from all this and spend the evening with Alan.

I felt oddly ashamed that I should feel like that. I ought to have had the guts to shove him out of my life, and take a chance on his damaging my career. That aspect began to worry me so that I couldn't concentrate on my written work outside the wards.

Alan's flat was all that I expected it to be. He let me in without a word, and went on mixing cocktails in a scratched but still efficient shaker. He watched me fling off my coat, with a lifted eyebrow, and barely grunted when I said I hoped he was better since he came out of hospital.

He poured me a cocktail and came over to sit beside me.

'Why didn't you come before?' he demanded.

The whole thing had a terribly nostalgic effect on me and took me back three years, to the time well before all those distressing events happened, to when I was running around with Alan and a lot of other young people rather like him. We had too much money to spend, and were rather unmannerly in the way we spoke to each other, a sure sign that we prided ourselves on being smart and modern. To insult a friend was considered more modern than to praise him.

'Couldn't,' I said, briefly.

'Why?'

I stared into his scowling face. 'Went home,' I told him, and watched him darken with anger.

'What's the idea?'

'Aunt Berenice asked me to. I had a week's leave.'

'If I'd known that, I'd have been there to pick you up, the minute you left Bardmore's,' he growled. 'When d'you qualify?'

'I told you – I've got another year at Bardmore's.'

He considered the point, and offered no comment on it. Alan was clever. He did nothing to offend me that evening. We had another cocktail, cigarettes, a few records on the radiogram, and then we went to a little place round the corner for a meal. It was the sort of meal Alan used to know how to find, and it was as different from anything which David could provide, as could be imagined. Alan had met a lot of the old friends and he brought me up to date with facts about them. He seemed to divine that it didn't mean an awful lot to me, and that my world was now in the hospital. Still he went on, talking in that clipped, yet entertaining way of his, knowing that I was listening against my will. One doesn't entirely jettison an old way of life, and old friends.

'What are you going to do, Alan?' I asked, at length.

'Stay around, till I get the itch to go on again,' he said, squinting thoughtfully at me. 'What are *you* going to do, Linda?'

'Become an S.R.N.' I told him quietly.

He shook his head. 'No. You're coming with me, when I get sick of being in England.'

I laughed at the total unexpectedness of that remark.

He raised sardonic eyebrows. 'Think not? I'm going to Central Africa, I think,' he murmured, and grinned as my interest showed unmistakably in my face. 'Or South America. I haven't made up my mind. You know, Linda, you and I are pretty much alike at rock bottom. Itchy feet. Can't stay put.'

I made to deny this, but he shook his head decisively.

'Don't you ever ache to know who or what your parents were?' he asked, and I winced as if he had flicked me across the face with a whip. 'Thought so,' he nodded. 'Wouldn't be natural if you didn't. We don't know, do we? Couldn't find out even if we wanted to. But get this, my girl. They must have been pretty much like my parents, when you come to think of it. All the signs are coming out in you now. Don't deny it, you know it's true as well as I do. Look at you. I ask you, it is natural that after the life you led at Marleigh, that you'd take a dip into this nursing racket! As if you'd stay in it, anyway. But it's the different aspect of it that got you. Same as me. We've got to stick together. We'd get places.'

'What makes you think I'd want to be in the same places as you, Alan, at the same time?' I asked, coldly.

'Because you came over tonight,' he chuckled. 'You didn't know for sure that I'd take the risk of putting you away, but you'd a fair bet that I would. I don't know whether I would, either, come to that, but it's a fair risk, taking it all round. Ah, stop looking like your poisonous foster-father and be matey,' he said, suddenly. 'Remember, old girl, the fun we had, before you started looking at me as if I was a bad smell?'

I did remember, and he saw it. I cursed my face for giving away all my secrets, and I cursed myself for only having the one way of hiding things from people – that way which meant I built an invisible wall round myself, and earned their dislike from the start.

'Do you know why I started going mad,

Alan?' I asked, softly.

'I always wondered,' he mused. 'You were such a snooty little devil till you were seventeen, and then you suddenly became real fun to be with.'

'No, not really fun. I just went a little insane, I think. I had a shock. I discovered I wasn't really a Fane. Just a no one. *Less* than a no one. I took it badly.'

He gaped for a second, and then swore softly under his breath. He coloured, too, and I guessed that he didn't like the truth of all that. He must have thought that he was responsible for changing me. That I had succumbed to his sinister charms, I suppose.

He said, leaning towards me, 'How did you discover that?'

'I heard you say something to my father, as a matter of fact,' I told him coolly. 'My father answered you curtly, but his reply left me in no doubt that I wasn't related to him at all. I never liked him, but it isn't nice to suddenly feel you aren't as much a relative as the worst of the–'

I broke off and bit my lip. Even to Alan I couldn't be so ill-bred as to voice my thoughts.

'Hangers-on?' he asked, with a twisted smile. 'Don't mind me. Hard words never hurt me. It's the holding back of the family purse that hurts me most.'

He insisted on taking me back to the

hospital gates. I couldn't shake him out of his decision, but happily he didn't wait until we were in full view of the building before he kissed me. He did that well in the shadow of the old plane trees, in the road before we came to the hospital.

And while I was shaken, inevitably, and cursing myself for it, he said, in a low, hard voice, 'No other boy-friends, understand, Linda? That is, if you don't want a scene.'

'Now when were you ever the exclusive man-friend?' I asked, lightly.

'Times have changed,' he said, and left me.

A strange, unsatisfactory evening, and one that would inevitably be the fore-runner of others, unless I could tell him to go to the devil.

I lay flat on my bed that night, as far removed from sleep as I ever had been. Even the ambulance bells didn't disturb me but remained a muted sound at the back of my consciousness, while I tried to thrash out just how much being a nurse meant to me, or whether I could bring myself to call Alan's bluff and lose everything.

Chapter Seven

It was possible, of course, to get transferred to another hospital, but when I pursued that avenue of thought, it would seem that that was no great possibility, after all. Matron would naturally want to know why, and I could no more find a convincing substitute for the real reason than I could give her the real reason in the first place.

My head ached intolerably by the time sleep finally came, and I had reached no satisfactory conclusion. I decided I would see David and ask his advice. If I could steer him away from what to him seemed a good alternative to a nursing career, then I might get some really constructive views on the subject.

Meantime Frances and I found ourselves with coinciding duties, and it was good. We had two quite bright juniors under us, too, and we were put on maternity. I was specially glad about this last general posting, because it meant that I wouldn't have to see Nigel on my wards, and to be spared that super embarrassment was indeed something.

Before we took up our new duties, other nurses of our particular grading had caught on that something was in the wind.

'Have you had a secret date with the gorgeous Armstrong, Linda?'

'Do you know him outside the hospital?'

'The way he looked at you is enough to make anyone swoon, but all you do is to go red as a peony and scowl!'

And so on. Frances parried the chaff for me as much as she could, but she was getting rather curious herself by the time we were sent to the Maternity Wing. It wasn't Nigel's manner so much as my own which gave rise to so much comment. He merely smiled pleasantly as he did to Sister, or indeed to anyone else who did him the smallest service, but I simply couldn't behave as if I had never seen him before.

I don't suppose the others really meant that they genuinely thought I knew him outside the hospital, but it was a good line, and could be reckoned on to raise a laugh whenever things got stale. I hated the idea of anyone getting a laugh out of it. That week at Marleigh began to rate simply as a very precious memory. I didn't suppose I should ever have the opportunity of speaking to Nigel again, let alone dining and riding with him.

Maternity was interesting. There were at least five extremely difficult cases, besides several waiting mothers in a small ward on their own, under observation.

Frances hated the observation cases. She always got in a muddle with the objectionable business known as 'ins and out'.

'Wouldn't you think that they'd drink the blinking water, instead of messing about so,' she muttered to me one day, as she measured urine in the sluice and entered it on the special charts. 'Golly, if my kidneys went back on me, I'd swim in the stuff if it'd do me any good.'

'They never do like water to drink, the kidney cases,' I murmured vaguely, checking my own tests.

'Look at this one, then! Where the deuce did it all go? Linda, it can't be right, she must have been telling me whoppers. She just couldn't have drunk all that. Look here. Intake five quarts. Urine test two pints.'

She looked at me with comical dismay.

'It's you, you dope! You've just forgotten to enter your bedpans,' I told her, in exasperation.

'On my honour, I'd have forgotten dozens, to account for that discrepancy, and even I couldn't do that. It's that junior. She's been mucking about with these charts.'

One of the really bad cases was a rhesus negative who had had five miscarriages and was still hoping. This time she had gone three weeks beyond her time. Every time I approached her bed, she would smile brightly, and say, 'I had a slight pain this morning, Nurse. Do you think that means I've started?' and would search my face with pathetic eagerness.

Sometimes when Frances and I were making her bed, Frances would tell her about mythical cases we had had, which were so much worse than hers. A wilder imagination than I could ever hope to achieve, sprang to her aid, and little Mrs Marks would listen wide-eyed, finishing always, 'And it *lived?*'

Frances always cheerfully assured her that there had been a happy ending, but I could rarely speak on those occasions. It struck me as being too heart-breaking, wanting a baby so badly that you had to go through all that, with so little hope.

'What d'you tell her all that bunk for?' I asked Frances, wrathfully, one evening, as we went off duty after tidying the beds for the last time before the night staff came on.

Frances looked curiously at me.

'If you don't know, then you're not in love and you never have been.'

It sobered me. It shook me, too. I had experienced the wild excitement of Alan's love-making, but so far, I had never been through anything which made me yearn to have a baby.

We never had to handle the infants, beyond taking them from the nursery, three in each arm, to the wards, at feeding time. The midwives bathed and bottle-fed them, and did the dressings on the umbilical cords. It was our unenviable job to wash nappies, clothes and bedding, and from that un-romantic angle, babies were just bundles of boredom to me. There is nothing particu-larly lovely about new infants, between one and fourteen days old. Until their fond mothers bear them off triumphantly in a foam of lace and exquisite knitteds, to their homes for the first time, they are just red-faced, squealing, wrinkled little objects dressed in what appear to be clean rags, and they are usually wet at both ends.

The mothers, however, were an absorbing topic to me. Frances and I were detailed to assist in a straightforward birth the first day we were on Maternity, and I wished it had been a difficult case. As it was, Sister Ronson and one of the midwives did it. Sometimes the medical students did the job on their own. One student and a couple of nurses. When it was a bad case, however, the houseman did the job, and while I was on that ward there was a case so bad that one of the honoraries, a famous gynaecologist, was called. It was an induced birth, and the child wouldn't come.

The mother was a highly nervous type, and every time the students trailed in after their honorary, and ranged themselves round her bed, you could almost feel her panicking.

Her eyes were filled with apprehension as she listened to the questions put, and the sometimes exceedingly silly answers. Sister Ronson used to get furious about that questionnaire within the patient's hearing, and after a series of battles, managed to get the honorary to take his 'firm' into a far corner to discuss the patient. But in little Mrs Butler's case, that did nothing to help. If she couldn't hear what was being said, she lay there imagining, until she was shaking like a jelly.

A joke was circulating round the hospital, starting with Mrs Butler's panic. We had two honoraries visiting the maternity wing at that time, and the younger of the two was rather more important than the other one. Mrs Butler didn't know this, of course. She preserved a hostile front to them both, and the fact that Mr Milson, the senior of the two, had a misleading geniality, and Mr Crane, the younger, had an acid wit, in no way helped things.

Starting with the usual castor oil and hot bath routine, after three days she was a white ghost of her former self, and still nothing had happened. Mr Crane invited his 'firm' to suggest other methods, and Mrs Butler lay writhing at some of their bright ideas. Then the waterbag was artificially broken, but the flow stopped. Milson pulled his weight the next day by starting the injections, and after a weekend of them, still with no result, she was near collapse from vomiting. But according to Mrs Butler, Mr Milson had said to his students in her hearing that a toxaemic case couldn't be operated on, because the conditions wouldn't permit a general anaesthetic. After a few days rest, Mr Crane came round, bustling and witty, and told Mrs Butler that as she would produce her child herself, he'd have to get going with his 'little bag'. Sister, knowing that Mrs Butler was already worried over a premature birth at seven months, had already explained this procedure, so that she shouldn't be frightened. Oddly, Mrs Butler wasn't scared, since she had been prepared for that rather unpleasant operation, but she convulsed everyone by indignantly asking why Mr Milson hadn't told the great Mr Crane that a toxaemic couldn't be operated on, anyway.

Frances took it all very badly. She confided in me one night on the way to her home, that every time she looked at Mrs Butler, she saw herself as an expectant mother. I had a sinking feel that things could be a great deal worse if Gordon Evans jilted her after all.

'Oh, Mrs Butler's an intelligent type, and if only they'd appeal to her reason, she'd be all right,' I comforted. 'She just wants to know about everything that's happening, and I can't say I blame her.'

'Yes, but that baby's going to die,' Frances wailed.

'How do you know?' I retorted, not very convincingly. 'In any case, if she'd come in at the very beginning instead of at this late stage, she would have had all the latest methods, and none of this discomfort.'

Frances said, under her breath, 'I wonder. Toxaemia gives me goose-pimples. They say they know all the answers about it, but *do* they? No one knows what causes it, *that* they all admit. And how can you cure a thing when you don't know its beginnings?'

'Yes, they do. It always happens when there's been anxiety during pregnancy. Mrs Butler's people worried her silly. She said so.'

'They're guessing at that cause, and you know it,' Frances insisted.

'Anyway, the patient's all right, once the placenta comes away,' I went on.

'Yes, if she survives that long!' Frances retorted. 'And look at Mrs Marks. She was actually saying she'd beat Mrs Butler to the Labour Ward yesterday! How about that for grim humour? Want to take a bet that neither of 'em'll survive, let alone their offspring?' and her eyes were glistening.

'Oh, I think we're both over-working,' I comforted her, as we got off the bus at the top of her road. 'What about the toxaemic twins? She had toxaemia and she was rhesus

103

negative, and both the infants tipped the wrong way round and came out feet first, but the whole three of 'em are alive and kicking.'

'Oh, that woman! She came from peasant stock, tough as nails,' Frances said, hardily. 'But look at Mrs Butler's constitution, and Mrs Marks' for that matter. Oh, lord, what did I want to try and become a nurse for?'

'Try being the operative word,' I said, lightly, and we were laughing as she let herself into the house.

Mrs Blake came forward to embrace us both. 'Linda, dear, we haven't seen you for such a long time,' she said, and in any other woman that would have sounded gushing. She had a trick of emphasising words so that the meaning was doubled, and I often felt that it wasn't possible for her to care so much about me, unless, of course, she imagined that David would succeed in bringing me into the family.

I looked round for him, and saw him in the kitchen, looking very domesticated, with a tea-towel tied round his middle, helping young Barbara to wipe up. Mrs Blake followed my glance, and said:

'Go through and see him doing something to help for a change, and you might tell Barbara I want her, will you, dear?'

I didn't, of course. The last thing I wanted was a tete-a-tete with David in the kitchen, but he kicked Barbara out, without any help from me.

He put the tea-towel down, and unfastened the one round his waist, as he said slowly, 'I didn't know you were coming, Linda.'

'I didn't know myself, David, but at the last minute Frances insisted.'

'You have to be forced to come here now?' he queried.

There was an uncomfortable silence, as I recalled how we parted. I was to get in touch with him the minute I got back from home. I had forgotten all about it.

I flushed shame-facedly.

'I didn't get sorted out, after all,' I told him miserably. 'The only thing I did discover was that nothing at my home could make me want to be a nurse less than I do.'

He nodded.

'That means that Torringfield is still on, I suppose?'

I looked sharply at him.

'David,' I said, slowly, thinking, 'David, I could be thoroughly unprincipled and say yes, I'll marry you, and leave you to sort everything out for yourself. I wonder what you'd do then? You don't even know the whole situation, do you? You've never asked me if I was guilty of any of those things it was suggested I was, two years ago. You just put blinkers on, and kept asking me to marry you. I wonder just how much you think you love me?'

'You couldn't take in the fact, I suppose, that I might love you despite anything you think you've done,' he murmured.

I shrugged impatiently. 'That isn't all, David,' I pointed out. 'You may not realise it, but I'm so tired, so sick and tired of it all, that I'm frightfully tempted to say, okay, I'll marry you, and leave you to deal with Alan. Oh, don't look like that – I'm fairly certain you could deal with him all right, and I suppose there are worse things than Alan's getting me kicked out of Bardmore's if he dared. I don't know. I just don't know anything, I can't think any more. I've gone round and round in circles, and I'm completely bewildered and sick, sick of the thought of it all. Only–'

'Only what, Linda?' he asked, quietly, watching me.

'Only I think you'd be sorry later, much later, at a time when I'd got used to the idea,' I said slowly.

He took me in his arms and stared down into my eyes. I still had my outdoor things on, and it was hot in the kitchen. The hot water tap was still running, and something was boiling over on the stove, and I suspected that the whole family were waiting rather impatiently to hear the result of our tete-a-tete before Mrs Blake could come out to dish up supper.

'There's something else, isn't there?' he persisted.

'Supposing I fell in love with someone else?'

His face twitched a little, but he said levelly enough, 'That would be the risk I'd take, wouldn't it? Anything else?'

'I'm a foundling. Don't know who I am. Might have criminals for parents,' I muttered.

'Go on. That isn't all, is it?'

I shook my head.

He said tautly, and I don't think I'd realised the depth of that leashed emotion of his until then, 'I think I could bear anything except that you'd been Torringfield's mistress.'

It wasn't like David to voice things so bluntly, and it was something of a shock to me.

I went a little limp against him, and laughed helplessly. 'Oh, David, knowing me, at least you seem to think you do, fancy saying that. Of course there wasn't any such thing, not with Alan nor with anyone else. How could there be?'

His face eased out again. Relief swept him, I fancied, but he was still bothered by the thing, the elusive thing, that was making me hesitate. In a weak moment, I wondered why I had raised the point at all. But after my having raised it, David wouldn't allow me to let it go.

'All right,' I said, wearily, 'it's this. Illegitimate isn't a pretty word, David. Even if you didn't care, what would your family say, if and when they found out, as I suppose they would at some time, that I'd been ... involved in a slander action?'

Chapter Eight

His mother came out at that point. Apologetically, and rather pleased at the sight of David standing holding me so rigidly that even at the sight of his mother, he forgot to let me go. There we were, in the midst of over-boiling saucepans, and wasting hot water, standing there, locked, tense, exceedingly unhappy. The unhappiness in our faces possibly escaped her, as she rushed to repair the damage we had done by our thoughtlessness, and by the time she had turned round, we had broken apart.

I said, 'I'll go upstairs and take off my things,' and David, after one last long searching look, turned round suddenly to the sink, and absently began making further inroads in the wiping up.

That wasn't a particularly happy evening. There was a telephone call, and Frances rushed out to answer it. She was a long time gone, and when she came back she looked as if she had been crying. David had nothing whatever to say, and sat apart from me, and young Barbara was left to keep up a bright flow of chatter.

We didn't stay the night at the Blakes. We

had had our quota of late passes for the month, and we tore off at the last minute as usual for our bus. There wasn't time for David to say much, but Mrs Blake said, as she wished me goodbye in his hearing, 'You will be coming again soon now, dear, won't you?' and I took that to mean that she supposed us to be engaged, even though we hadn't said anything. She was a good soul, and regarded young people as crazy but utterly lovable, and took all their vagaries in her stride.

Because there wasn't much time to spare, and because I suddenly had the insane wish to really be engaged to David, I said, 'You'd better ask David that,' and left him to sort it out himself.

Frances said, as we got on the bus, 'Is it all mucked up between you and Dave?'

It wasn't like her to ask a direct question, and I rather wondered what had provoked it.

'I'm not sure. It does rather depend on David,' I said carefully. 'How about you?'

'That was Gordon ringing. It's all off,' she choked.

Of course, I had expected that, but not quite so soon or in so dramatic a way. I thought it rather mean of him to ring her at her home in her spare time, but perhaps he thought it more discreet, especially if she was going to be upset, than if he had done it in the hospital.

'It's nothing to do with me,' she said, with difficulty. 'He says he still cares for me, only his great-aunt, who's financing him, doesn't want him to be married till he's "arrived". He's got to be absolutely free, she says, and she holds the purse-strings.'

It didn't sound convincing to me, but I made all the appropriate noises, and encouraged her to talk.

She had been to his home, it appeared, and met his uncle, with whom he lived. There was a housekeeper, and evidently plenty of money. The old lady, who was really wealthy, lived in the country, but came up periodically to see Gordon, and to have a talk with the uncle, who was supposed to be keeping an eye on him. The uncle wasn't the type to enjoy such a role. He was a casual, free-and-easy sort of man whom Frances had rather thought liked her. Unfortunately he, too, was rather dependent for his luxuries on the old aunt, and when pressed, he had admitted to her that Gordon had been getting a bit more friendly than usual with the current girl-friend, and this little nurse appeared to be staying the course.

Frances said that rather bitterly. 'That's just how he *would* phrase it. He made me feel like one of a succession of weekend girl-friends just at first, till he got more used to me, and then he treated me with a bit more respect. Honestly, I thought Gordon was going to announce our engagement. But if that's how much he cares—'

She didn't mean that, of course. If he'd altered his mind after that, and suggested holding on, and persuading the aunt to view the thing favourably, Frances would have still hung on. I knew it, she knew it, and I think she despised herself for it.

'That's how it gets you,' she choked. 'He's the only thing that matters. I wouldn't care if the whole hospital went up in smoke – oh, don't look so shocked. I mean that. I wouldn't care how much my people loathed the idea, and I think they would, if they knew. Even they're taking a back seat. It's only Gordon who counts, and I don't care how he's treating me.'

'Is that what the "real thing" is really like?' I marvelled. In hospital, the 'real thing' was discussed more than anything else. Love was the only antidote for perpetual illness and disease all round us. It went in various grades, from mere flirtations, sky-larks between student nurses and medical students, to heavy crushes on honoraries. It was all the difference between a proudly sported engagement ring and a deep and furtive affair behind closed doors. It was the thing that led to marriage and children, or the thing that led to a nice arrangement of cash and choice leisure for the rest of your life. It was companionship or the more violent emotion. There were no end of facets to it, and all were aired, discussed, approved of, sympathised with, according to the merits of the case. But whatever the brand or ingredients, it was Love with a capital L, and the only thing worth talking about. And the so-called 'real thing' sat at the top of the pinnacle.

Everyone agreed that it meant suffering, which had always amused me up till now. To talk in a hushed voice of suffering in connection with the most desirable thing on earth, struck me as being ludicrous when we were surrounded with suffering of various kinds. And now Frances had taken the plunge right into the middle of it, with me close on her heels, for even if I wasn't bitten by the bug myself, I was in all the interesting processes of it.

'Wonder what it's like to be like Verrens?' I mused suddenly. Verrens was a Staff Nurse, and the only things she thought of, talked of, and lived for were Efficiency and Duty. She was very, very good at her job, but not for much else, so far as I could see. She was flat-chested and angular, and hadn't even the quality of a pleasant voice. To live to be a nurse seemed rather a limited existence, much as I wanted the vocation.

'You wouldn't believe it, but she's got her troubles,' Frances said, edgily.

'What, old Verrens?' I gasped, scandalised.

'They say she had a husband once, even if she doesn't wear a wedding ring any more.'

That was such a facer to me that I lapsed into a tight silence, which neither of us broke till we were back in hospital.

We undressed and prepared to fall into bed, when I remembered I'd left my tooth-paste in the bathroom. I padded along to get it. It wasn't only a question of tidiness and breaking rules. Tooth-paste cost money and might easily vanish.

The bathroom on our floor had the fire escape running past it, and my heart turned over as I saw a dark figure crouching on it.

I hastily put the light out and went over to the window, half guessing in that second who it was.

'Alan, what the blazes are you doing here?' I breathed.

He helped me push the sash up, and said curtly, 'Looking for you.'

'Suppose I hadn't been out here? Or someone else had been taking a bath?'

He said impatiently, 'I had to take a chance. I know your room number, and if they'd changed it, that'd be just too bad for you.'

'Well, now you've found me, Alan, what d'you want?'

'Money. Let me have some, but quick.'

I felt sick. It was like rushing through

space, back over twenty-four months, to all the old sensations and memories. Alan looking over his shoulder, the old furtive look in his eyes. And that old familiar demand. Money. In those days I'd had a large allowance to help him out with. Now it was different.

'Don't be stupid. I haven't got a bean. We're not paid till next Tuesday,' I protested, and he had the sense to believe me.

'Haven't you got any in the Post Office?'

'If I had, I couldn't help you with it now,' I pointed out. 'What have you been doing, Alan?'

'Never mind that. I want some, that's the point. Borrow some from your pal, what's-her-name.' He looked ugly and added, 'I'll ask her if you won't.'

Alan had taught me to think quickly, where he was concerned. 'What's it for? Fares?' I breathed.

'You don't suppose I want it for the telephone booth, do you?' he retorted. 'Listen, I know a man who'll give me a passage to Amsterdam, if I can make the boat in the next hour.'

'Wait there. I'll see. How much do you want?'

'As much as you can get, of course,' he said.

I pulled down the window, leaving him outside, and he made no attempt to stop me. I had got money. I still had some of my birthday money, and although I had hoped to put it by for emergencies, to get rid of Alan out of London for even a little while, was something.

Frances said, 'Where've you been all this time?' and stared at my hands, which were black from the outside of the window. 'Where's the tooth-paste you went for?'

I stared blankly. 'Oh, damn the tooth-paste,' I said. 'Frances – I do hate this, but – can you lend me some money?'

I expected her to say she was broke, the instant I had said it. But I suppose her un-happiness over Gordon had sharpened her perception. Instead, she said, quietly, 'Get-ting rid of Alan?'

I nodded, and rummaged in my bag, finding close on five pounds. Without a word, she turned out her notecase, and found another five.

'If this means helping our David,' she said, irrelevantly, and shoved it at me.

'If by helping him, you mean presenting him with me as a wife, I suppose it is,' I said, shakily, and pelted back to the bathroom.

When I got back to our room again, I knew I'd have to tell Frances something about it, since she'd helped me.

She said, as an opening gambit, 'Did you get rid of him?'

I nodded. 'Thanks for your loan.'

She stared curiously at me. 'You know, I'll never get to know you really,' she said, slowly, 'and oddly enough, I can't stop liking you. I thought I hated you not long ago, when I saw what you could do to our David, but now I know I don't. You get people, like a disease. Can't help liking you, and I suppose that's how it'll always be.'

'Thanks,' I said, dryly.

'I don't even care if you go all distant and snooty,' she said, wearily. 'I want to talk to you. You see, only because of Gordon, I can begin to see what our David's going through, over you. What's it all about, Linda – why don't you cut free from that Torringfield man, and marry David? You know he's crazy about you!'

Normally I'd have been very angry and told her to mind her own business, but I could hardly do that in view of her loan, and asking no questions at the time.

I shrugged. 'David's got it badly over me at the moment,' I said, slowly, 'but will he always have? I'm trying to put it to him that he may very well regret marrying me, in time. I wouldn't like that.'

'You care for him that much?' she said, eagerly.

'Blessed if I know. No, I think it's just that I admire him so much as a person, that I wouldn't like his life to be ruined because of me. You know, the ordinary feeling one would have for a friend.'

She nodded, and looked disappointed. 'But why d'you suppose his life would be messed up by marrying, since he seems to want that so much? Our David's a good judge of character, and when he knows what he wants, he just hangs on until he gets it. Like that last commission of his.'

'What commission?'

'Hasn't he told you?' she gasped.

'He never talks about his work,' I said, still thinking about Alan. 'He's always discussing us and our future.'

Frances said, 'I wonder why he hasn't told you? It means so much to him. There's a lot of money in it, too, and publicity. You know he gets regular commissions most of the time, now, don't you? Not just hit-and-miss freelancing, I mean.'

I didn't know, and I could hardly see that it mattered.

'That means he's making good money, and has been for some time,' she persevered. 'He'd flay me alive for telling you, if he hasn't, but I wanted you to know. I mean, well, you might think perhaps he couldn't afford to marry you and all that, seeing that you come from wealthy people, I mean–' and she broke off, flushing.

'You didn't want me to marry David some time ago,' I said, slowly. 'What made you alter your mind?'

'I don't know,' she said, at last. 'It's crept up on me. I don't think I quite know how; it's just all tied up with being treated badly by Gordon's people, and seeing David so miserable, and not being able to loathe you as I thought I should, when I first heard about that rotten business you were in two years ago. Linda, can't you tell me what it was really about?'

'Not all of it,' I said, flinching, as always. 'It's all tied up with Alan Torringfield. He's a sort of distant cousin. No, not really that, since I'm not related,' I said, half to myself. 'Anyway, he was always in trouble, wanting money, cheating at cards, debts, all that sort of thing. I was so used to it, I thought nothing of it. I was so bitter in those days, it gave me a savage sort of pleasure in being friends with the family's bad-hat.'

I looked at her, and she had the same kindness in her eyes that her mother had sometimes. Frances in a gentle mood was a lovely person. I wondered how on earth Gordon Evans could bear to hurt her as he was doing.

'Funny to be bitter with so much money, and no need to work,' she mused.

'There was a reason,' I said, shortly. I played with the idea of asking her how she'd feel if she found out suddenly that her parents were perfect strangers and that she didn't even know who she was, and then I

119

decided against it. It wasn't worth it. I wouldn't be able to stand the kindness and sympathy which would pour from her, and I'd be furious when I found that same kindness making her tell everyone within reach what a rotten deal I had. No, secrecy at all costs.

'It's all right, David knows about it, and he says it doesn't matter,' I assured her abruptly. 'Anyway, because of this, I played the fool and kept friends with Alan. He got caught out, doing something pretty low, and my people took him to court over it. The blighter told them I was involved, and they called off the case, but not before the newspapers got wind of it. That's all.'

She looked doubtful. 'As a matter of interest, *were* you involved, Linda?' she asked, smiling, obviously very nervous of the reception of that question, but at the same time needing very badly to know the answer.

'What do you think?' I asked, curiously.

Still smiling, she said, 'I'd lay a pretty big bet that you weren't involved at all, but that you were too stiff-necked to say so.'

I gasped, as she put out the light and lay down, chuckling. 'Linda, I can say all this in the dark, because you can't intimidate me with that high-and-mighty stare of yours. I wish you'd be nice to our David, as nice as you can be. He's so very much in love with you, he'd wipe out all the unhappiness that's gone before. After all, if he thinks it doesn't matter, all that old business, I'm sure he's right. And I think you care for him more than you realise. I think it's possible to be in love without knowing it. We aren't all made alike, and maybe it's as well.'

I didn't answer just then. I couldn't.

'Mother and Daddy like you so much, too,' she went on. 'They don't understand what this is all about, but I know they'd love it if you and Dave fixed it up. Honestly, this nursing business is all right when you're young, but it's not much cop when you get as old as Verrens, for instance. Fancy getting up in the cold grey dawn to look after a lot of strangers for the rest of your life, when you might devote your energies to someone who really matters to you!'

'It's a good thing Matron can't hear you, Frances!'

'We're being honest for once,' she said, quietly. 'How far away has Alan Torringfield gone on our life savings, and what proof have you got that he's gone?'

'Only that special look, when his mind had already taken him faster than his feet ever could, away from the scene of the crime,' I told her. 'He mentioned Amsterdam. That's far enough for my peace of mind for the moment.'

She didn't press the point any further, but

in the silence that followed, I could almost hear her beseeching me to fix things up with Dave, and shove Alan out of my mind.

As it happened, I had very little chance to do much about it for the next few days. Suddenly little Mrs Butler began to have labour pains, and Mrs Marks produced some new symptoms, too. It all boiled up at once, and we seemed to have little time to think.

Mrs Marks was sitting at dinner one day, with the rest of the mothers who'd had their babies and were getting about. She loved those meals with them, and talked hopefully to them about their babies. She was always cheerful, and her rather thin high voice could usually be heard above the rest, asking questions as if it was a dead certainty that this child of hers would live and she'd need to know everything for its welfare.

Suddenly she went red as a beetroot and hurriedly left the ward. I found her throwing up, in the bathroom.

'I don't know what's the matter with me, Nurse,' she gasped. 'I felt all right, when all of a sudden—'

That was the beginning. Thereafter she complained of a pain high in her side.

That afternoon the husbands visited. I don't think I shall ever forget the look of joy on the faces of the Marks, who both thought that they'd soon be parents. Nor will I forget the look of agony on Mr Butler's face, watching his wife in strong labour. While he was by the bedside, another injection was administered. They were two-hourly, and irrespective of persons or conditions. Even if Mrs Butler was asleep, they lugged her awake, and plunged the hypodermic into her thigh, already peppered with angry red spots.

When we went off duty that day, Frances said, 'She's had it, of course,' and she was referring to Mrs Butler. But next morning we found that Mrs Butler had had a small, but very strong little baby in the night, and was pretty well considering. Mrs Marks, however, had been rushed off to the Labour Room at the same time, and had been unconscious in less than an hour, and delirious. I saw Frances staring at her empty bed with a dazed expression on her face. Mrs Butler was in another ward, and sleeping comfortably.

Mrs Marks was wheeled back on a stretcher, a couple of hours later, and left alone in the little ward in which she and Mrs Butler had spent so many hours together. She lay in the centre bed, with an empty one on each side of her, but at that time she neither realised her lonely state, nor cared.

There was an influenza epidemic at that time, and we had quite an outbreak of natural premature births. In most cases, the babies didn't survive, owing to the virus attacking them at an early stage. Some, three and a half and four-pounders, were popped into the oxygen tent as soon as they arrived, and the girls seemed to struggle through. The boys, however, made no effort.

There was a young mother of seventeen in there, who contributed to Frances' harrowing days in Maternity. She had a three and a half pound boy, who seemed to be defying all the normal laws and was hanging on to life. At four days, there was the general feeling that he would pull through. Whenever anyone came from the special nursery where the oxygen cases were, she would say, 'How's my Half-Pint?' with her cheerful cockney grin. One day it was the medical student Greenway, whom she asked. Bill Greenway was terribly conscientious, in his last year, and rather too tender and kind for a doctor, I thought. He had brought her boy into the world, and his face was tortured as he bent over her, and told her quietly and kindly that her little baby had collapsed, a few hours ago.

Wherever we went in the wards, you would find a young mother sobbing under the bed-clothes, having lost a baby. It was beastly. Sister Ronson used to send them home at five or six days, cautioning them to stay in bed when they got there, but believing that it was better for them to be away from sight and sound of other people's babies. Mrs Butler was always crying because her little baby was too small to suckle, and she hadn't much milk. Expressing the milk is a painful business at best, when there isn't much there, and she soon found out that her baby would die if it kept sleeping and wouldn't take its food. The emotional balance is more often than not, upset to a marked degree in pregnancy, and I sometimes wondered if I was quite sane when I left that batch of crying mothers and found Frances, in our room, crying over Gordon.

I wished, above all, that Sister Ronson would send Mrs Marks home. I went in alone to tidy her bed one day and found her sitting up, a blank expression on her face, staring down at her hands, across which lay several skeins of white wool.

As she saw me, she called up that determinedly cheerful expression to her face, and said brightly, 'I thought I'd make up some vests for myself, Nurse. No sense in wasting the wool, and vests are always useful, aren't they?'

I agreed that that was very sensible, and looked down quickly, concentrating on my task.

But she wouldn't let me escape as easily as that. 'Nurse, I've never found out what happened. You'll tell me, won't you? No one else will. I don't know why, I'm pretty sensible, and I'm used to it by now, having had five misses.'

I never knew why they persisted in calling miscarriages 'misses' and it vaguely irritated me.

'Oh, well, you know, we can never tell what makes these things happen. Better luck next time.'

It was inadequate, but I couldn't tell her the truth.

'That's what I say to Albert,' she agreed, 'but he says he doesn't know what to think. I heard that doctor say to all the students that each time you have a baby, being rhesus negative like me, the chances get slimmer of it coming off.'

I agreed with her that this was so.

'But that doesn't make sense, Nurse, does it, seeing that so many rhesus negatives get born, and then they drain the blood out of them, or something, and pump rhesus positive blood back, don't they, and then it's all right? How d'you make that out?'

'Who told you that?' I smiled.

'Sister explained it to me before the baby came,' she said firmly, and my heart sank. 'So I don't see what went wrong.'

I couldn't say that it was during the night that the baby tilted, and that her sort of breach birth couldn't be a success. There is a tradition in Bardmore's that the mother's

126

life must be saved at the expense of the child's, so they had removed the child and saved Mrs Marks.

'I was wondering if I'd done it myself,' she went on, looking searchingly at me. 'See, I know it was a "bridge" birth. I heard one of the doctors say that if you don't keep taking pills every day, the baby tips upside down because it hasn't enough room to come properly, and, well, I said "yes" to the chart when I ought to have said "no", because to tell you the truth, I was a bit browned off with running down the passage all hours during the night, those pills do play the devil with me so,' and at the end of that incoherent recital, she burst into hysterical tears.

'I don't think you did it yourself, Mrs Marks,' I said firmly, and did what I could to quieten her, promising myself that on pain of death I wouldn't go into that little ward again on my own. I didn't dare think what Sister would say, if she knew that Mrs Marks had added herself to the list of patients who listened in to the honoraries talking to the students within earshot.

Frances said, on our next time off, 'Let's get out of here. What shall we do this afternoon? Flicks?'

'All right,' I said, without enthusiasm, and allowed her to pilot me to the newest, noisiest, most garishly-coloured musical in Town, during which Frances went into gales of hearty and no doubt beneficial laughter at the sections of slap-stick comedy with which the film was peppered. I was very tired when we went back to her house for supper, and I wondered if I was wise in running the risk of seeing David again. It wasn't easy to slide out of it, however, since I had nothing else to do, and I didn't want to offend her nice mother, who had cooked, especially for me, a meal which I had once rashly said I liked. Frances announced this 'surprise' with satisfaction.

It was a week since I had seen David. It was odd that he hadn't tried to get in touch with me, and I could only assume that he hadn't been able to stomach that last remark of mine, in the kitchen, when his mother had come out and unwittingly interrupted us.

He wasn't in when we arrived. Mrs Blake said that he had had to go and see the editor of one of the big dailies, about some new work, and she had sounded very pleased.

It was strange without David there. I realised that I had never been in that house before, without him. I looked round the big living-room with new eyes. It reflected that family so much, and all of a sudden it seemed a very nice place to be in. There was a solid feeling behind it all. The big roll-top desk in the corner, which belonged to Mr Blake, and where I had seen him sitting sometimes, going over family accounts and entering up in his little books. Sometimes he brought work home from the office, and sat going up and down long columns of figures, totally oblivious of all the row and laughter, and radio music, going on in the room around him.

There was a very dark carpet, mainly reds and browns, I noticed, and heavy curtains at the windows, of much the same colour. All the warmth in the world seemed centred, that dank foggy night, in those curtains and carpets, and in the cheerful blaze of the log fire. The furniture had a fat look. It was mahogany, much polished, and the big round table, used for meals and everything else, had a fellow shine on it, and like the chairs and the sideboard, had bellying legs also shiny and comfortable-looking.

Everyone in the family had their photographs on the mantelpiece, walls, piano top and indeed anywhere where there was space for a frame to stand or hang, and they were all pleasant, worthy people, like the group of Blakes I had come to know. The radiogram alone was kept free from pictures, but that was because it was always being used. Records spilled from the big shelves by it, and there were filled bookshelves, with books spilling over and put in hasty piles on the very top. A comfortable, not too tidy room, with all the difference in the world from the places in which Alan spent a sketchy existence. All the difference in the world, too, from my home, with its gracious drawing-room, its books in the library where they ought to be, its dining-room and its morning-room. Aunt Berenice would be shocked at all this. She would complain, in her sweet, gracious voice, that the lack of style and taste disturbed her spirit.

I pondered that apparently frivolous sentiment, and then I decided that it wasn't so frivolous as it sounded. It might be the truth. Aunt Berenice would probably be extremely unhappy in such a room as this. But then she wasn't the earthy type that I was. I suddenly realised just how earthy I was at rock bottom. Stripped of all the polish, the conventions, the ides of other people, that was part of my life at Marleigh Park, I realised that I hadn't really got any taste of my own. I had no really personal convictions about any of the things that formed my background. I had accepted them, they were all that I knew, until I found this. This dear room, which spelt mainly solid comfort and security.

I hadn't noticed Mrs Blake and Frances go out to the kitchen. Barbara had been careering around trying to find some books she had lost, and she, too, had gone out without my noticing. Only her father remained, sitting quietly in his own chair with its high old-fashioned headrests, puffing at his pipe and watching me with a half smile, and a quizzical expression.

'Now what do you think of it, lass,' he murmured.

'Think of what, Mr Blake?' I stammered.

He waved his pipe-stem in a circle embracing the room. 'This room. This house. Us. You were thinking pretty deeply about it all just then.'

'I suppose I was,' I said. 'I felt as if I was seeing it all for the first time.'

'Not much compared with Marleigh Park, eh,' he murmured, quite without rancour. Rather as if he were debating.

I didn't answer. It seemed to me a nice subject for a debate, but not a relevant subject so far as I was concerned. There were other things which mattered too much, such as stripping myself of everything which had been given to me at Marleigh, and then discovering myself as I really was. That strange, lost orphan, with the unknown parents, who didn't know where she was going. Who was haunted by Alan Torringfield and loved by David Blake; who was chasing nursing as a career because of two doubtful reasons – conscience, and a need to do something which would provide a home and an escape.

'Is that what puts you off, lass?' Mr Blake pursued, quietly.

I brought myself back to him with an effort,

and found myself saying, in an exhausted voice, 'I'm not sure I am put off any more.'

It was not Mr Blake who answered that, but David, who stood at the open door, his face ashen, his lips moving soundlessly. And then he said, 'Linda! Do you mean that?'

Chapter Nine

He came across the room to me, and pulled me to my feet. Mr Blake went out of the room, and thoughtfully closed the door behind him, but it didn't matter. Nothing mattered beyond this new discovery, that I wanted – for some reason which I couldn't yet divine – to be here, and to belong here.

'Linda?' David murmured.

I nodded. I hadn't any words. As far as my own feelings to David were concerned, nothing was changed, and I felt a cheat. He believed I had discovered I loved him after all. His mouth, tenderly yet eagerly, told me that, because I felt so rotten about it, I even tried to return his kiss with a little warmth. But it was good to feel his arms around me. Safe, somehow. I knew just how much I needed to feel safe, that night.

David murmured, looking tenderly down at me, 'When did you find out you cared, Linda?'

I didn't answer to that, but said instead, and in a rather shaky voice, 'David, I thought you wouldn't want to see me any more, after that last time, and my gruesome confession. Especially when you weren't here tonight.'

He smoothed my hair, and looked at it, and at my eyes, my nose, my mouth, looked at every feature, and then at me as a whole, just as if – as with me and this room such a little while ago – he was seeing me for the first time, and finding what he saw very good.

'Silly little brat,' he murmured, fondly. 'Mind you, I don't say I shall like it an awful lot if you go in for that sort of nonsense again,' and he laughed, or tried to.

We were both rather incoherent. He tripped, getting me over to the worn settee, and we laughed about it. I stammered, trying to talk rationally, and we laughed about that, too. And then he started talking about an engagement ring.

'You've boggled at the idea before. I hope you won't be, well, difficult now, Linda, because,' he said, still trying to laugh. 'I don't think I could bear it if you chucked the poor thing back at me again,' and he got out the little case rather shame-facedly.

'Do you carry that about with you–' I began, painfully, but I couldn't go on, after catching the expression on his face.

'I stick, you know,' he said, thickly. 'I get an idea, and there it is. I know what I want, and I batter my head against all sorts of obstructions till I achieve it. I'm like that. Stolid, I suppose. Can't help it.'

'Oh, David,' I said, helplessly, and I was

rather near to tears. He was so nice, so very nice. Why on earth couldn't I take a header for him, as so many girls would? All the time I felt so inadequate, and not particularly honest. I was painfully conscious that what I had to offer him was so very much smaller than all the abundant love he had for me.

'David, I won't refuse it, but don't mind, my dear, if I don't wear it. At the hospital, I mean.'

'Why?' he asked, quietly.

'Oh, I don't say nurses don't wear engagement rings, though it is an awful nuisance, having to take them off every time you do a dirty job, or dressings. No, it isn't that, only–'

'Let's have it,' he said, quietly.

'If Matron hears of it,' I said, desperately, 'she'll think I'm the same as all the others who just grab at nursing as a way of getting a husband. I know it sounds rotten, but some even marry patients. It isn't that they all have such ulterior motives. They might just happen to meet someone and fall in love, and marry before they finish their course of training, but you know what Matron is. You can't convince her that they really had nursing at heart at the start. And I did. I want to finish my training, and I don't want her to know about this.'

He looked puzzled.

'But you've got over a year yet, haven't

135

you, Linda?'

'Yes, just about,' I admitted.

'Well, what's the point of finishing your training, if we're going to be married?'

'David, dearest, I'm the sort of person who must finish something she's started. Besides, I might need it some day and wish terribly that I'd qualified. Who can tell?'

That point he appreciated, and as I expected, he gave way at once.

'But I want it understood,' he insisted, 'that you don't work when we're married, once you've finished your training.'

'Well, I can't go rusty,' I murmured, but he swept that aside.

'If you ever need to take it up again, I imagine you'll soon be able to brush it all up. If you can't remember what you've learnt in these three years, you won't be much of a nurse, my dear.'

And there I had to leave it. But there was another point which had to be cleared up, before his nice family came rushing in to bless, congratulate and generally yearn over us.

'What about your people knowing ... well, all about me?'

David frowned.

'Look, Linda, I don't usually keep things from them, but I think we must be sensible, and not tell them about what happened two years ago. They wouldn't understand ... I don't quite understand myself, but never mind. I've accepted it, because you mean so very much to me. I can't ask them to accept it blindly, in the same way. Does Frances know anything about it?'

'A bit,' and I told him about our talk, the night we got rid of Alan. He didn't like that a bit, and said we were both a pair of young fools, but as we'd done it, nothing could be done to undo it.

'But Linda, promise me, dearest, if he ever comes back and bothers you, don't meddle with it. Tell me.'

I promised. In that sort of situation, one promises anything. 'What about me being, well, not a Fane?'

'We won't tell them that either,' he said, and he seemed relieved that Frances hadn't yet been let into that secret.

He pulled me into his arms again, smiling. It had been a typical inquisition and settlement, that brief question-and-answer session, and I think we were both a little amused by it, in a rueful way.

As he kissed me, a long lingering, singularly sweet kiss, he murmured against my cheek, 'I wonder if you'll ever know just how much I love you, Linda?' and it seemed prophetic. I wished he hadn't said it.

I was still clutching the little leather case in my hand, and he looked at me rather curiously.

'Linda, do you realise? The first time you saw that, you just flinched from it and I put it back hastily in my pocket. In the park. We neither of us mentioned it. Now you're just holding it. You haven't even ... seen it.'

I flushed, and opened the case, expecting the conventional single diamond. Instead, I found a beautiful ring with three sapphires set in a row.

'David! It's ... utterly lovely!' I whispered.

He nodded, slowly. 'I wanted you to like it,' he murmured.

'Oh, David, and that first time, I didn't even open the case,' I said, brokenly.

'Don't stand staring at it, darling. Try it on. I guessed your size,' he said, but his voice was rather uncertain, too.

It was a little large, but not a bad guess. David said he'd have it altered. We'd have to go to the shop and try on the size card with the holes in it. It sounded a little silly and I giggled, and then young John poked his head round the door.

'I say, whenever you two get together, it always mucks supper up. I'm hungry!'

David put his arm round my waist, and said, 'Tell your mother it's all right.'

John grinned. For fifteen, he was a tall lad, but there was an engaging air of tender youth about his face that was endearing. He scuttled off to the kitchen, and then the family surged in.

There was a great deal of fried skate and chips that night, I recall, which struck me as rather incongruous, till I reminded myself that David and I had been blowing hot and cold over our engagement for so long, that his mother could hardly be expected to plan a suitable meal for the date when it was finally settled. Afterwards we ate custard tart, which she made extremely well, and there was excellent coffee.

I remember the details of the food as well as I recall every other detail of that evening. They accepted me so wholeheartedly that it made me ashamed, especially as they apparently took it for granted (with perhaps the exception of Frances) that I was in love with David.

They were going to give us an engagement party, and were disappointed that it couldn't be at Christmas, because both Frances and I were on duty then. They wanted to discuss, right away, the wedding, the sort of place we'd live in, the furnishing of it, and the date. All the usual excitement and discussion about a first marriage in the family.

David pressed my hand beneath the table, as if to say, 'Let them have their head. Don't deny them this,' and so I said nothing, beyond reminding them, as I had reminded David, that I would want to finish my training. Oddly, they accepted that. They, too, didn't care for something so big and important to be left unfinished.

It was David's father who threw a spanner into the works.

'Now how about your people, lass? We've heard about your grand home, but we'll have to meet your folks, of course. We're simple people, and they'll have to take us as we are. Eh, David, lad?'

I froze with horror, but oddly it was the eyes of Frances that I found myself seeking, not David's.

There was a deeper despair in hers, beyond the set frozen smile on her face. She was, I realised, thinking of Gordon Evans and his up-stage family, and of how this might very well have been a discussion about her own wedding, only it hadn't come off.

I heard myself saying, in a far-away kind of voice, 'Well, you see, it's a little difficult.'

'Oh?' Mr Blake said, in a questioning sort of voice.

I met his eyes with a courage I didn't really feel. 'My father,' I said, firmly, 'is not an easy man to get on with. Not a bit like you, for instance. Frances could come to you with things that bothered her, and talk them over, and even if you were angry, it wouldn't matter, I imagine. Now my father–'

'Yes?' Mr Blake prompted, gently, but I saw that he was not to be put off. He was going to do the right and proper thing, if it killed the lot of us.

'–is rather strong-minded,' I said, feebly. 'You see, he gets an idea, and he can't see anyone else's point of view. To be honest, we didn't see eye to eye over something nearly three years ago, and well, the fact is, we haven't spoken to each other since. Haven't seen each other.'

'Well, lass, isn't it high time that such an unsatisfactory state of affairs was put right?' Mr Blake smiled. 'Surely now is the time to do it? Go to him and tell him you want to be married, and you can't be happy with things the way they are with him.'

I stared hopelessly at him, and wondered what he would say if he saw my father as I had seen him last, standing in riding breeches and hacking jacket, back to the great open fireplace in the library. The dogs were with him, and sensing their master's mood, they bristled at me. My father was holding his crop in a way that suggested to me that if I were a boy, he would thrash me with it. And the coldness of his eyes was not of anger, but of an active, unaltering dislike. It would be there for ever. I was not his, I was merely imported into his home to please his wife, when they lost their own child. To such a man as he was, I imagine that that fact alone must make him as bitter as gall.

But Mr Blake didn't know that, and he added to the fire. 'You don't think it would work, Linda? What, his own flesh and blood?'

That about finished me. I bit my lip fiercely, and I couldn't look at David. I was only conscious of Frances, sitting staring at me in horror, because she had never seen me upset, but always calm, with the single exception of that night in our room at hospital, when I had almost thrown her out. Obviously she didn't want a repetition of that performance, and I suddenly realised that my being upset was working havoc on her, considering how miserable she was already.

She suddenly said, desperately, 'Shut up, Daddy! Leave her alone! Can't you see it isn't the time or place? Oh, heavens, how this wedding talk makes me sick!' and her face suddenly crumpled. She got up, scraping back her chair, and fled from the room.

'What's the matter with her?' young John asked, his mouth open, and blank astonishment in his eyes.

Mrs Blake got up. 'Really, it's unforgivable of Frances. I'll go and find out–'

'Please, Mrs Blake,' I said, urgently. 'Don't go to her. Leave her alone for a bit. She'll be all right.'

She looked at me and sat down again. 'Do you know what's the matter with her, Linda?'

I nodded. 'Don't mention it to her, anyone, please. She didn't want anyone to know, but I think I ought to tell you. She's been jilted.'

In a way, it took their minds off me, and I

managed to forget my own misery in telling them as much as I dared, without disclosing who the man was or where he came from. They were in turn, shocked, angry, commiserating, and rather hurt that they had known nothing about it. Especially David.

'I don't think it's all that bad,' I said, treading carefully, 'only just at present we're hopelessly over-worked at the hospital, and hospital work gets you down in a funny sort of way. If you're not careful, you take the patients' troubles personally, and it's doubly upsetting,' and I plunged into an account of some of the cases we had at that time, without getting too technical.

I didn't hope to hold their interest, but oddly enough, they were absorbed, even young John, who wanted to be a doctor but hadn't much hope because of the expense involved. By the time Frances came back, they were all listening intently to my account of the case we'd had in Women's Surgical before we'd been switched to Maternity. There had been an accident case transferred from Casualties because of suspected internal injuries, which particularly interested young John, because of the number of limbs she had broken, and the way they were all strung up to the ceiling.

'You're a horrid boy,' I told him. 'You remind me of one of the honoraries who isn't interested in a patient unless there's a maximum amount of damage done.'

In the general laugh, Frances slid back into her seat. She didn't look too bad. She'd evidently bathed her face in cold water, and made up again, and brushed her hair until it shone, and she was determinedly bright. In a way, she suddenly reminded me of little Mrs Marks, just before she had been sent home. It was pathetic, that ghastly courage.

Mrs Blake kissed me fondly when we said goodbye, and Mr Blake took my shoulders in his hands and gently squeezed them.

'I don't need to tell you, young woman, that I'd like you to feel free to come and talk to me, if you want to, sometimes?'

Anyone else would have hugged him, I suppose. He was so nice. But I couldn't. I could only nod, and whisper, 'Thank you,' but it seemed to satisfy him.

David walked with me to the bus, Frances hanging behind at home until the last minute, as usual.

He said, looking quizzically at me, 'I suppose you couldn't bring yourself to tell me the name of the man who–'

'–jilted Frances?' I said, swiftly. 'No, I couldn't, David. You see, she still loves him, and I think he cares for her. The reason was, well circumstances. I think, I've got a sort of a hunch that it might be put right. But it needs finesse, and in your present mood, you'd take a hatchet.'

'Who's going to use the finesse?' he wanted to know.

'I thought of having a go,' I said, doubtfully. The thought had only just come into my head, and I wasn't very hopeful.

'Good girl,' he whispered. 'When am I going to see you again?'

I liked that. The way he had quietly left it to me to help Frances. As if he had such confidence in me.

'My next free time,' I rashly promised. 'And don't let me catch you wasting precious working time, hanging about the hospital for me when I come out for a couple of hours.'

When Frances joined us, and we clambered up on top of the bus, she said abruptly, 'You told them, didn't you?'

'Did your mother say something, then?' I asked wrathfully.

'No, but you had no business to tell them!' she flared.

'I didn't mention names or professions,' I said, 'but it was either telling them a bit about it, just generally, you know, or else letting your Mother go dashing out after you, and demanding to know what was up.'

She took that in, and had the grace to look ashamed.

'Sorry,' she said, shortly. 'I just hate them to know I've been thrown over, that's all.'

'Frances,' I said, hesitating, 'how d'you feel about me – David and I getting engaged

– now, after it's really happened?'

'Fine,' she said, briefly.

'Oh, good. Because there's something pretty personal I want to put to you.'

'Not about Gordon!' she said, quickly.

'About Gordon,' I insisted. 'Do you, in your heart, honestly believe he cares … enough, I mean? What I'm trying to say is, it really is only his old aunt, and not him, at the back of it all?'

She nodded, still angry at my suggestion.

'Well, couldn't something be done?' I asked her.

'What, for instance, apart from waving a wand or working a Christmas miracle?'

'Don't be bitter. I was only thinking in terms of string-pulling. If it comes to that, surely that's better than you savaging yourself like this. If you both care enough, I was just wondering whether the old Marleigh Park crest might work the oracle on old Auntie.'

She turned and stared thoughtfully at me.

'How?' she asked, at last.

'Oh, well, you know, Aunt Berenice might be persuaded to make Gordon's aunt's acquaintance. Sure to be a mutual friend who could manage it. They're both in the same county, aren't they? I think you said so. And then Aunt Berenice could invite us down, and mix the clan well together. You know, dear little Frances is my niece's best friend, and all that. So you'd be acceptable.

146

Sorry to put it so bluntly, but you know Gordon's aunt better than I do.'

She looked strangely at me.

'Wouldn't it be more to the point to say, "Dear little Frances happens to be the sister of that nice young David Blake who is going to marry my niece? Didn't you know". That, surely would be what your Aunt Berenice would say, isn't it, Linda?'

She had me there, and she knew it. I hadn't any intention of telling Aunt Berenice about my engagement to David, not yet, anyway.

I didn't answer. That one was hard to get out of.

'And what about your father?' Frances persisted.

'What about him?' I asked, sullenly.

'Is he away, or something? Because if he isn't, I don't see quite how all this string-pulling is going to take place, if all you've said about him is true. He doesn't sound the sort of obliging person who'd have that kind of thing going on in his house.'

'All right. We'll call the whole thing off,' I said.

'Why aren't you going to tell them about David? Isn't he good enough?' she persisted.

'I didn't say I wasn't going to tell them. It's just plain awkward, since I'm not on speaking terms with my father. It wouldn't matter who I was marrying, I couldn't do anything different.'

147

'What will your aunt say?'

'I haven't the foggiest.'

And then, like her father, she dropped her spanner into the works, only it was worse than his.

'Do you really intend to marry our David, or are you just fobbing him off by getting engaged?'

Chapter Ten

It was our stop then, and in scrambling downstairs I hoped that she would forget that I hadn't answered her question.

But she didn't. Frances never forgot an unanswered question, if it was important enough to her. She took it up when we got back into our room, and there was no wriggling out of it.

'I'm not in the habit of starting things I've no intention of finishing,' I said, coldly.

'But you're not in love with him one little bit,' she accused, 'or else you wouldn't put off telling your aunt about him. He just isn't good enough for your high-and-mighty relations!'

'Oh, stop it, Frances,' I begged. 'I've told you how I feel about him. For all I know, it might be as much as I can feel about anyone. I'm certainly not in love with anyone else.'

She looked strangely at me.

'You might not be, but that isn't to say you won't be, one day. I don't believe you're so cold as you make out. I think you've just schooled yourself not to feel anything, or at least show it. But I think you'll go smack

149

into love for someone one day and feel just as badly as I do about Gordon. And then what's our David going to do? That's what I don't like about it!'

'Well, you wanted me to be engaged to him! You said on the bus that you felt fine about it!'

'That was before you said you weren't going to let on about it at home,' she said, slowly. 'That just about made all the difference.'

'I see.'

I sat down on my bed and thought about it. 'Not a very nice person, am I?' I asked her, with a turned-down smile. I was very tired of the way things kept going back on me. At David's home tonight, I had felt safe, even if my conscience did prick a bit. And then I got all the back-kicks, in those questions about home, and David telling me just what to hide and what not to hide. Life had been so very complicated since that night when, at seventeen, I heard the truth about myself. I wouldn't have believed anything could bite so deeply.

'No, you're not,' Frances said, bluntly. 'You're too darned snobbish and remote, and you tell lies when it suits you.'

We stared at each other, and then she sat on her bed, too, and held her head in her hands.

'That's what I know about you. That's

what I feel, and yet I can't let it make any difference. Oh, hell, isn't it all a mess? I'm as miserable as hell, and I think you are, too.' She suddenly looked up and started to laugh. 'The only one who's really happy tonight is our David!'

But he wasn't. I knew that, I who knew him so well. He was more at ease than he had been for a long time, and certainly relieved to think that we were at last engaged. But I don't think he would have been happy if we'd been married at that moment. He'd never be really happy with me, not until all this mess was cleared up.

We stayed in the Maternity Wing until well after Christmas, and I was rather thankful for that. Christmas is a very gay time in hospital, and it's always nicer to spend it with patients who aren't really ill. Last year we were on the Shakespeare and Bacon Wards, both adjoining, and filled with stomach cases. There was hardly one who hadn't had a major operation recently, and they could neither eat, drink, nor enjoy very much. They weren't allowed to laugh for fear of bursting stitches, and all of them looked so ill and white and thin, that Frances and I agreed that it was the most miserable Christmas we had ever experienced.

This year was fun. We set all the mothers on making decorations, and in each ward was a tree; tiny trees in the little wards, and a huge one in the general ward. Everyone seemed to have new and fresh ideas. One of the mothers knew how to make huge spiky balls of coloured paper by twisting it round a pencil end and screwing the paper tight. She made loads of them, in two and three colours and threaded them with string for hanging. Jacob's Ladders and paper chains, silver stars from tea paper, long fringed streamers of crepe paper, all came out of that resourceful little ward. Another small ward made fairy dolls from cotton wool and pipe cleaners, with wings of cellophane, and dresses of white crepe paper.

Some of the visitors brought quantities of metal milk caps and from these were made stars and flowers strung on to coloured embroidery silk. One little mother who was still waiting for her child, took her mind off her troubles by making a crèche, a thing of beauty, coloured with poster paints which her husband brought, and lit from the roof with a couple of small electric torches.

We had carol singing, of course. At midnight on Christmas Eve, and first thing on Christmas Morning we had a singularly beautiful church service, held in the largest ward, and all those who were able to leave their beds, came, even if they were wheeled in a chair.

'A white Christmas,' I found time to

mutter to Frances, in passing, and looked back from the window where great clots of snow were whirling past outside, to find her eyes like stars.

'I say, are you all right?' I asked anxiously.

She nodded, and scurried off to the sluice. I followed her and she thrust a small box at me. It was a velvet case containing a fine slender gold bracelet set with what looked uncommonly like rubies and pearls.

'To match my ring – he wouldn't take it back, you know,' she said, and after the slightest hesitation, thrust a note at me. 'I wouldn't show anyone else, but I wanted you to know.'

The note read, 'You may not believe it, but I'm still crazy about you, and if you can wait that long, I'll come back for you when I've "arrived".'

I gave it back to her, speechless.

'What do you think?' she breathed. 'It's a *wonderful* Christmas!'

'I give up,' I muttered, reflecting that there were still bedpans and stitches and urine tests, and a long and ardent letter from David which needed some sort of answer.

When we got our break, we went and lay on our beds and read our mail and poured over our presents again. David had sent me a beautiful leather make-up case with gold fittings. There were smaller gifts from his mother, Barbara and young John, but his father had shown more shrewdness than even I gave him credit for.

He had sent me a leather-bound copy of *Hazlitt's Characters of Shakespeare's Plays,* with the note: 'For my prospective daughter-in-law, who can never resist taking down my copy and having a peep.' I hadn't thought he'd noticed.

Frances got a lot of things from her family, too, but nothing mattered so much as Gordon's bracelet. She lay dreaming up at the leaden sky until we had to go back on duty, and I hadn't the heart to speak to her, and break up her dream. Alan's note was put hastily into the inner pocket of my handbag. Why spoil Christmas, I thought, with looking too much at that? After all, it was no new thing for Alan to ask imperatively for money. It was disquietening, none the less, to know that he was back in England so soon.

There was, also, a letter from Aunt Berenice, who appeared to be very disappointed at not hearing anything further from me about Nigel. She seemed to think that I would be sensible enough to further the friendship which she had so thoughtfully started for me. She again sent me a generous cheque, and said that my father would be going back to America at the end of January, for six months, and that I was to feel free to visit her as often as I liked, even for hasty weekends.

Putting together the letters from Aunt Berenice and David's father, I was stuck with a new problem. Both of them had tied me down to such different futures. I knew quite well that Aunt Berenice would be absolutely furious if she knew that I had got myself engaged to someone not personally known to her. She loved to matchmake, and as far as she was concerned, the old affair, though unfortunate, was over and done with, and with a bit of skill, she could still 'arrange' something for me. The fact that my father was still so hostile didn't worry her a bit. No doubt with her flair for management, she would stage the whole thing while he was away, and she would bask in the glory of the producer and backer, just as if the whole thing were a very well-received play. To see me settled with someone of whom she approved, would, I perceived, wipe out a lot of the feelings she had had for me, to which I could never pin a name. Hardly remorse or conscience, not perhaps even sorrow, but something of all three. I was an orphan, a no one, taken into the family and brought up as someone, and then thrown out at the first unfortunate hint of instability.

She did not, I was sure, feel responsible for me, but at the same time, she would feel a great deal better if she could settle my future for me. It was a nice point, and in no way derogatory to her. It was the way she had been brought up to look at things. I daresay that if I could have heard her views, heredity meant a great deal more to her than even I thought it did, and environment less than nothing. I daresay also she strongly disapproved of adopting unknown children, and that I had been nothing more than an interesting experiment, of whom she had grown very fond during the years, quite against her will. I knew, also, without being told, that the surest way to displease her was to go against her wishes, her cherished plans for me.

I put the problem away, and went back to the wards with an almost dazed Frances. Dazed with happiness this time. The first baby to be born that Christmas Day was a handsome little Greek girl. She received Sister Ronson's gift of a Savings Certificate, after the custom of the Maternity Wing. One year triplets were born, and Sister Ronson was never allowed to forget her expression when she came on duty and was told that she had to provide three Savings Certificates. The case was an unknown one, transferred from another hospital whose Maternity Wing was full up at the time, so it was a surprise all round.

Frances yearned over the new baby, and I could see that in her mind she was already married to Gordon Evans, with possibly his first child in her arms. It was a grizzly prospect that came to me at that moment; supposing Gordon Evans never quite 'arrived', or perhaps didn't become famous (and free to marry Frances) until they were both too old? I felt sick at the idea, and I thought of all sorts of hard things against Gordon Evans for sending her this gift and raising her hopes. To my mind it was more unkind than if he had left her as she was.

But how I could help Frances, I had no idea. Unless I conformed to the wishes of Aunt Berenice, I could hope for no help there – possibly not even then. She might thoroughly disapprove of a little unknown nurse forming an attachment for a man who might one day be a famous surgeon. That she had ideas about Nigel Armstrong and myself was rather different. I had at least been brought up as Nigel Armstrong's wife would expect to be. Where Aunt Berenice went wrong was in imagining that such a friendship could be furthered in hospital, and that amazed me. She was shrewd as a rule. If I'd still been at the Park, it would have been easy, but as it was I might as well have been at the other end of the earth.

There I was wrong, and Aunt Berenice so right. I was about to wheel out the trolley of tea-things when Sister Ronson rustled by, and catching sight of me, sent me over to the Women's Surgical Ward with a message for Sister Winston. I left the trolley for Frances when she came back off the ward, and scuttled over, confident in the knowledge that Nigel Armstrong would hardly be likely to be about at this time on Christmas Day. The honoraries, by time-honoured custom, attended for the carving of the turkey on their wards, and for the rest of the mid-day jollities, but by tea-time they could be expected to have vanished in search of more sophisticated pleasures outside the hospital.

I delivered my message, got the answer, and was scuttling back, when Nigel appeared from Sister's office, and catching sight of me, smiled blandly and bowed slightly.

'Ah, Nurse Fane, isn't it? How is your Aunt Berenice?'

I told him I thought she was quite well, and kept my fingers crossed in case Sister Winston should come rustling out of her ward.

'A charming lady. I haven't seen her since I was at Marleigh Park,' he observed. 'Give her my kindest regards when you write. Oh, and will you dine with me on Tuesday, at seven thirty– Yes. Splendid. I'll pick you up at the gates at seven sharp.'

Chapter Eleven

It was all done so neatly. With an almost curt nod, he had gone down the corridor, leaving me standing like a fool. I was not conscious that I had said yes, I would dine with him. I was only conscious of having stood with my mouth open and not a thought in my head.

Also I had forgotten the answer to my message. There was nothing for it but to go back.

Scarlet to the ears, I explained somewhat incoherently that I had slipped down in the corridor, and it had put the answer out of my head.

Sister Winston said kindly, 'As it's Christmas, I'll overlook it, Nurse,' and obligingly repeated the message.

This time I got back without mishap. Sister Winston, I recalled, with gratitude, was the person who had made me first look at a dead body. I had been very new at the time, and the first day on her ward I had blanket-bathed a very sick patient, under Sister's eye, and only a few hours later I heard she had died.

'Have you seen anyone dead before,

Nurse?' she had asked, gently.

I hadn't, and although I had prepared myself for it I found it filled me with horror. My father hadn't let me see Mother and in some way this first dead woman was oddly tied up with Mother.

'No, and I don't want to, not yet,' I said. 'Next time, please.'

'I think you'd better get it over now,' Sister said, and took my arm, leading me behind the screens. Mother had only been dead a few months, at that time, and to my fevered imagination, it was her face I was looking at, and not Mrs Brown's at all. I went stiff as I stood there, and I was conscious of Sister's hand tightening on my arm, as if in support. Then my vision cleared, and it was only Mrs Brown, and she didn't look any different from when I last saw her. Just as if she were asleep, only much whiter.

I said as much, and I also said thank-you, and Sister Winston appeared satisfied.

Now the immediate question was whether to tell Frances, and then David, about this dinner date with Nigel. Frances I ruled out at once, because in her present overjoyed state, her tongue would run away with her, and it would be all over the hospital. David was a more sticky problem.

I lay thinking most of the night, trying to be honest, and at the same time trying to do what would be easiest all round. Not a very easy task. In the end, I decided not to tell David. After all, he wouldn't be happy about it, naturally, and if there was never another invitation from Nigel, where was the sense in upsetting David for nothing? David, I reasoned, would never understand that in our world a dinner date meant nothing.

I pondered on the point about Tuesday. How did Nigel know it was my next time off duty, without having gone to the trouble of looking it up?

Frances said she wanted to stay in next day and mug up her last lecture notes. We were due to go on ops. again soon. She loathed the operating theatre, and still – after many visits – came over queasy when the first incision was made. So I went out alone.

The snow, which had been so utterly beautiful and seasonable over Christmas, was now melting, slowly, messily, as only a London snowfall can. It was a cold thaw, too, and I shivered a little and smartened my pace. Someone set his pace beside me, someone with his overcoat collar turned up, and his felt brim pulled well down.

'Alan!' I breathed.

'Hallo, there!' he said, cheerfully, and a quick searing relief flooded through me. He was muffled against the cold this time, and not against recognition.

'Where are you off to, Linda?'

'Nowhere. Just a walk.'

'How long have you got?'

'Two hours.'

'Come to Glaseby's. I'll buy you a drink.'

'Glaseby's! You must be prosperous.'

'That I am! Forget my last gentle request for financial help. Tuck it away in the old tin box, and remember me next time I'm in need.'

'Just the same, you ought to know I can't go and have a drink anywhere, not while I'm on duty.'

'Go on. It's a restaurant. We'll get a meal and split a bottle, then.'

It was early for lunch, but I fell in with his idea. I think it was mainly curiosity. There was a certain excitement about Alan's ups and downs. There always had been. That, I reasoned sadly, was an off-shoot from my dubious roots.

'Has life been exciting?' I asked him.

He hailed a cab and bundled me in, and in the brief space of time before we drew up at the ornate entrance of Glaseby's, he put in quite a bit of useful spade-work with his usual brand of kissing.

'Alan,' I said, trying to keep my voice steady, 'what would you say if I told you I was going off being kissed in taxis?'

He let me thrust myself away from him without protest, and chuckled. 'Suggest somewhere else to show my affection,' he said, with a grin.

Nothing, it appeared, was going to worry him unduly today, he was on top of the world, and very engaging.

He knew how to order a meal, too. I sat back and luxuriated while he discussed wines with the wine waiter, and summoned the head waiter to order our meal. And then he said, suddenly,

'When's your next evening off?'

'Tuesday, and it's booked,' I said, grinning saucily at him.

His face didn't darken as usual. Perhaps it was my own manner which caused him to pause, and wait for an enlargement of that.

'With our most important honorary,' I told him, adding with satisfaction, 'I'm afraid, Aunt Berenice fixed it.'

Alan said, 'Oh, I see. Um, that's very interesting. How far are you going to push it?'

Just for fun, and without any real thought at all, I said, lightly, 'All the way, naturally!' and I was horrified to see, by Alan's expression, that he approved, and was working out just where he could cash in on it.

'Now wait a minute,' I began.

He laughed, and leaned back.

'You've got me on your hands for keeps, girl, you know that. I'm on top today, so I'm being nice to you. You'll be on top next week, and then you'll be nice to little Alan. Jolly good partnership, that!'

I thought of David with a sinking heart, and was only very grateful that I had Nigel to thrust in as a buffer. I could make Nigel my excuse when I was seeing David. I don't know what made me come to that sudden conclusion. I felt instinctively that Alan was impressed enough with Nigel's importance, so that he would not smear his name when he spoke of him. He would encourage me to see Nigel. I saw that. But with David it was different. I knew that if Alan got hold of David's name, he would be beastly when mentioning him. He would speak sneeringly of him, to say the least, and he would certainly prevent me from seeing David if he could.

I don't know why I felt protective of David's existence, where Alan was concerned. It was all instinctive. I was moving about just then in a fog, not really reasoning at all, but acting purely on instinct.

I said, suddenly, 'If you're so flush at the moment, how about refunding the money I borrowed from my girlfriend that night?' and to my intense surprise he did. He got out, with the utmost amiability, a well-filled wallet and repaid me the whole amount, mine as well. I didn't bother to tell him that some of it was mine, in case he altered his mind. I took it all in silence.

Lunching with Alan was a curious business. He wasn't smart or well-groomed, and yet there was something about him which got him respect and service. He knew what to order and how to order it and he did it with a careless assurance that I could only admire. He had a rollicking laugh, and he didn't care who heard him. He let his admiration for me shine out all over his face, and made me feel that I belonged to him, and I didn't like it, but there was no altering Alan.

He took me back in a cab, with just a minute or two to spare and just when I was afraid he was going to take me in his arms again, he leaned towards me and said, with an impudent stare, 'So you don't like being kissed in cabs, Linda? O.K, you shall thank me for this lunch next time we meet,' and he laughed in a way that made my face scorch, because I caught sight of the taxi driver half-turning, and grinning.

That was what was so hateful about Alan. Whether he didn't want to go any further with me than he did, or whether he intended to at a later date, I shall never know. But he managed to make other people think that he was going all the way, and that was almost as bad.

I was rather afraid he would be lurking about on Tuesday evening, having changed his mind, or merely with the intention of upsetting me just before I met Nigel. But if he were lurking around, I never saw him.

Nigel drove up in the big black car just as

I came out of the main gates of the hospital. Frances had departed earlier for home, with the idea implanted in her head that I was dining with one of my aunt's friends, just to please my aunt. She said 'Poor you, don't be too bored,' and I promised I wouldn't, and hated myself. I prayed that she wouldn't forget something and come back just as I was getting into Nigel's car.

Nigel said, 'Punctual. Good girl, Linda,' just as if no intervening days and weeks and months had gone by since the last time he had said that, during that lovely week at Marleigh Park.

I glanced sideways at him, and saw that the official blandness, that slightly mocking air mixed with authority, which I disliked so much about him in hospital had slipped away, and he was his old easy self again. Confident, yes. He was terribly self-confident, but then one would expect that.

We dined at one hotel, went on to the next for dancing, and finished up with a cabaret. He smiled at my obvious enjoyment, and said calmly, 'I knew you'd enjoy the evening I'd planned. I know your taste very well.'

'How did you know? Did Aunt Berenice tell you?'

'She didn't have to. I watched you pretty closely during that week at Marleigh. You did like my company that week, didn't you, Linda?'

There was the faintest shade of anxiety in his voice, and it seemed an odd thing for him to say. I didn't understand it then, but I did later.

'Of course,' I said.

'I thought so,' he agreed. 'I found it the most enjoyable week I've had for a long time. You'll dine with me again?'

I wanted to, terribly, but I didn't see how I could. If I did it again, I'd have to tell David.

He didn't appear to notice that I hadn't answered at once. He took out a small diary and consulted it. 'Your next evening off duty doesn't come until Thursday week. Arrange to change with someone next Tuesday. I'll pick you up at the same time.'

I was flabbergasted.

'But I don't know if I can!' I protested. 'Oh, I'd like to very much, but supposing–'

He raised his eyebrows, as if thoroughly surprised that I couldn't arrange time off just when I liked.

'I want you to meet my mother. She's staying with me. She'll dine with us, and then there's something very important I want to discuss with you.'

And there it was. He had arranged it with almost regal precision and brevity, and I couldn't think of anything to say against it. To say that my fiancé would think it odd if I went out with a surgeon at my hospital would sound almost like blasphemy. The great man wanted the little nurse to dine with him. What did it matter what her boyfriend thought? But would David take it like that?

I wanted to giggle at the absurdity of the situation. I was so much imbued with hospital procedure that at that time I did not see Nigel as someone likely to court me, despite Aunt Berenice's famous arranging tactics. He was just the most important honorary to me, and there seemed little wrong in it.

So much so that when David met me on my next free mid-day break, I told him about it. On the spur of the moment. I said that it was a nuisance because he was a friend of Aunt Berenice, and I couldn't very well refuse, since he was also one of my own superiors, and David seemed rather amused.

'Don't tell Frances, though,' I cautioned.

'Why?' he wanted to know.

'Two reasons. One, she's so soppy over her own affair, she'd probably blurt it out all over the hospital, and not even notice, and you can just imagine how awful that would be for me. Two, I have a wild idea of asking the great man to help Frances.'

I saw my mistake the minute I'd said that. David pounced on it at once.

'Is the man she's in love with, a doctor,

then?' he asked, sharply, and looked displeased.

'Oh, heavens, now the cat's out of the bag. Yes, he is, and he's got a beastly relation who's financing him and doesn't want him to marry anyone at all until he's at the top of the ladder. I think if Aunt Berenice's friend could pull his weight, Aunt Berenice might be persuaded to do something, too, with the relations of Frances's doctor bloke, if you follow, and it might be all right. What do you think? You don't object to all that, do you, David?'

It was a little late to ask what his reactions were, but it was better than not asking him at all.

He said at last, 'To be frank, I don't like any of it. I never have cared for string-pulling, and I don't quite see how Frances will fit in, if strings are pulled. Does she know about what you're going to do?'

I was getting deeper into it and I knew it. I did the best I could. 'I sort of suggested asking Aunt Berenice to do something. You see, Frances's doctor's old aunt (bit involved, isn't it?) lives in my Aunt Berenice's county, and for all I know, they might know each other already.'

'And Frances?'

'She loathed the idea,' I said at once, and David looked pleased.

'Does this chap (whose name I notice I

haven't been told) really care for my sister?'

'Don't sound so beastly formal, David!' I protested. 'Yes, yes, he does care, I believe, very much.'

David grunted.

Then he turned round to me and said, very earnestly, 'Linda, my dearest, don't ever hide things from me.'

'Well, what a thing to say!' I protested, feeling guilty at once, as I always did when he looked at me in that deeply sincere way of his.

'I seem to have spent so long dragging everything out of you,' he went on, 'and I can't rid myself of the feeling that you'll go on not telling me everything, on the grounds that you don't think it necessary to, or don't want to bother me, or some such reason. The reason doesn't matter, but the fact that you do or don't tell me, matters to me such a lot. Do you understand that?'

'I have told you everything now,' I said defensively.

'Yes, eventually,' he smiled. 'But will you always? Can I rely on it?'

As I didn't answer for the moment, he went on, 'Won't you just come to me and say, David, I'm going to do so-and-so, do you mind?'

'But you might say you *do* mind,' I pointed out, 'and then I might not be able to do it.'

He laughed suddenly, joyously, and yet

tenderly. 'You *are* such a child, Linda, and I do love you so!'

That made me feel much worse than anything else he could have said. The feeling persisted, even when the following Tuesday arrived, and having told David I had to dine with the man and meet a relative of his, I still felt guilty. I just went on remembering that last thing he had said to me.

It didn't make any difference when David, like Frances, commiserated with me on having to spend an evening off in such a way, instead of having a gay time with him.

I dressed carefully, and asked Frances how I looked.

She said, with a curious look, 'Far too nice to go out to dinner with a friend of your aunt's and his old mother.'

Put like that, I agreed with her.

'Give my love to David,' I said, and for once I meant that.

Nigel's place was very much in the same category as Marleigh. Good taste and not very much comfort. To say anything flippant or crude would have been shockingly out of place, and I felt just the same about his very sedate man-servant as I did about our own butler. It was very aggravating but just that evening I felt I wanted to be at David's house, and if I didn't exactly want to let my back hair down, at least I wanted to feel comfortable, and not have to put myself back into the special skin I seemed now to keep for visits to the Park. It depressed me to think that during those years at the hospital, the thing that must be my real self had been gradually thrusting into the background all the careful exterior that had been built up from my birth. It was incredible.

Nigel's mother gave me a very careful, though well-bred look, smiled at me, nodded at Nigel, and murmured, 'Very nice. Quite charming, in fact,' and he seemed satisfied with her approval. She was very old, very gracious, and pretty much like an older edition of Aunt Berenice. As the evening wore on, I slid back into the old feeling I got at Marleigh, and I forgot about the Blake family. It wasn't very possible to remember them while Nigel was talking. He had a forcefulness about his personality, that blotted out everyone else and everything else. I found that what he was discussing, counted. I had to think about it, and take part in it. He interested me enormously.

After dinner, his mother said a gracious goodnight, and we went into the library, a magnificent apartment, where we discussed quite a number of things, until Nigel decided it was time to bring out – in his own good time – the subject of the evening.

'I said there was something very important I wished to talk to you about,' he announced.

I was leaning back in the chair facing him, with the light full on my face. It was softened rose-pink light from a beautiful glass shade on a lamp nearby, and it shed rosy shadows all over my cream brocade gown – which I bought with Aunt Berenice's Christmas money. I felt very well-dressed, and I had shed, for the evening, all the things that usually pressed in on my tired brain.

'Has any man told you he loved you?' Nigel asked, with nicely-timed shock tactics.

I blinked. It was the last thing I had expected him to say, and defensively, I said, 'Oh, scores of times.'

He smiled. 'I thought so. I don't intend to tell you that, personally. But,' he said, leaning forward a little, 'what I will tell you is, having considered you from every possible angle, I find you the most suitable young woman I have yet discovered to be the wife of a famous surgeon.'

Chapter Twelve

That, I found, was like Nigel Armstrong. He liked effect, he loved shock tactics, he never bored, and he had a ready and delightful flow of words which rather excused him for holding the floor for any length of time.

He told me, in a fair amount of detail, just what he liked about me. It seemed that I was not only, in his opinion, extremely good-looking, but rather unaware of it – a fact which tended to endear me to him. Modern young women, he found, were painfully conscious of any good looks they might have, and it bored him.

It went without saying, that I had the right background and connections, the right sort of schooldays tucked behind me, the correct manner for a surgeon's wife, and he added with a trace of puckish humour that I was even the right height – also important to him.

Finally, I had a nurse's training. At least, I would have, by the time I had my S.R.N. He didn't like surgeon's wives who were merely social butterflies. He wanted a wife who could share his passion for medicine, a wife with whom he could discuss his cases, and on whom he could rely not to be bored with an evening of work instead of an evening out. All this, he was sure, I agreed with. I had, also his tastes where art and music were concerned, horses and dogs, riding and the country. Perfect, in fact.

I listened in dazed fashion. Whatever preconceived ideas I had about him during that week at Marleigh, I had never imagined anything like this. He had seemed an ideal companion there, and no more. I think I jibbed at the business-like way he put all this to me. If he had told me he'd fallen in love with me, and then worked up to the rest, I might have felt better about it.

'Now, Linda, I don't want your reactions at this moment,' he finished. 'I see, with complete approval, that you're a good listener. You haven't interrupted me once. I like that. I want you to go back to your quarters and think this over. Take your time. And I believe I can rely on you not to mention this to anyone.'

'Of course,' I said, faintly.

He didn't ask me if I were already tied up with anyone else. He apparently took it for granted that I wasn't. And I didn't take him up on it. David was my business.

'You will dine with me for once a month,' Nigel went on. 'It's a set date, so there'll be no need for confirmation of it, or any discussion whatever, in hospital. (Unless, of

175

course, by any remote chance you don't wish to go any further with my proposal). Is that all clear?'

He said it as if there wasn't the remotest chance in the world that I shouldn't be ready to fall head over ears in love with him and pant to marry him, I thought angrily. Anger was my main emotion at the time, but a lifetime of training kept it hidden. I rode back beside him and left him at the hospital gates without a word. He merely said, 'Goodnight, Linda,' and formally shook hands.

Anger stayed with me most of the time, until I dined with him again. In all those four weeks, during that bitter, sleeting, January, whenever I thought of Nigel, it was only with anger. Fury, even, at times, to think that he considered I had no other chance, (even with Aunt Berenice behind me) than to snap up his offer.

I should have known that anger was a dangerous emotion to have about any man. If impatience and contempt hadn't mingled with my anger about Alan, that might have been dangerous, too, except that I knew Alan for what he was, and could keep him in that special niche where he could do very little damage to my heart. But it wasn't like that with Nigel.

Meantime, we were taken off Maternity, and attended regular lectures from the honoraries. These were interspersed with duty in the operating theatre. I liked it, personally, but I was always careful to station Frances a little behind me, so that if she was inclined to come over queasy, she could fall forward on me, and not against the inner ring, the people who were doing the operating. The thought of fainting against one of them always appalled me, and I wished with all my heart that Frances would chuck up nursing before any real disaster happened.

She didn't look very well these days. Operations really upset her. She said it was the heat and the smell of the anaesthetic, but I could almost feel her flinch beside me, as the incisions were made. She studiously looked away when the waste was flung in the buckets and when a limb was amputated, she lived in terror that it would be handed to her to dispose of.

'Frances, you shouldn't go on with it,' I insisted, every time we came out of the theatre, but it wasn't any use. I think she felt that Gordon Evans would think less of her. He often assisted Nigel, and I believe she felt that he could recognise her despite the theatre suits and masks, and despite his preoccupation in his task. Gordon Evans had that passion for his work which Nigel had. I used to like to see Nigel walking down the wards, Gordon at his heels, lapping up everything which Nigel said to him. Nigel wasn't upstage with his houseman, and I liked him for that. He often asked Gordon for his opinion, and listened courteously to it, and tactfully put the younger man right if he was out a bit in his conclusion.

Meantime, I spent all my evenings off with David. I don't know what happened to Alan at this time. I heard nothing from him, and I began to feel distinctly easier. I stopped worrying about my forthcoming marriage to David, and I didn't actively think much about Nigel's offer. There was just that searing anger there, whenever I recalled how he had taken me for granted, and I hoped that in time that, too, would go.

But I was wrong, and David was the one who pointed it out to me. One evening, his parents went out to see a film, a not very frequent occurrence for them, and Barbara was out, too. Only young John stayed at home, and he was in his room wrestling with his homework.

David had records on the radiogram, and absently put off the centre light, leaving only the soft glow of a reading lamp in the corner nearest the records. I was lounging in the corner of the settee, flicking over a record catalogue by the light of the fire, when I found David looking at me. Standing with one elbow on the mantelpiece, and a curious expression on his face.

'It's an old one,' he said.

'What is?'

'The catalogue.'

'Oh, well, it doesn't matter, does it?' I laughed, throwing it down.

'It might not have, if you hadn't been holding it upside down,' he said, gravely.

I indignantly denied it, but I couldn't say for certain whether it was the truth or not. I hadn't really been looking at it. I had kept up a pretence of going through it, so that David shouldn't talk to me.

'Don't watch me too closely, David,' I begged.

'Why not? You're the only one I want to look at.'

'I didn't mean look at. Watch, the word was, and you know perfectly well what I meant.'

He nodded.

'I feel as if you're taking the lid off my head and peering into my mind sometimes,' I confessed.

'And you don't like me to do that?'

I considered him a little more closely than I did usually, and I realised that he didn't sit close to me any more, and very seldom touched me. He sat down now on the settee, but it was at the other end, and although he lounged back with apparent ease, he wasn't entirely comfortable. Considering that we were alone, an engaged couple, with soft music and low lights, and an air of intimacy in that comfortable old room, we were being

179

rather formal.

'I don't like anyone to do that,' I said at last.

'And yet, you know, Linda, it's of paramount importance to us both. Is Torringfield worrying you again?'

'No. I haven't seen him for some time. Why?'

'Someone's making you angry,' he told me, quietly.

'Have you thought that it might be you, David?' I countered.

'No, it isn't me,' he said positively. 'You don't think about me enough to get angry with me. In fact, you don't always see me.'

'David, that isn't true!'

'Yes, it is, Linda, and don't trouble to deny it. You can't help it, my dear. You see, I took a risk in getting our engagement announced. I know you don't love me. You said so. You were honest about it. I just hoped and prayed that some day you would come to love me. But a chap in my circumstances must of necessity be always on the watch in case some other chap comes along. No one can help falling in love. You can't prevent yourself from falling in love, I mean. If that happened to you, Linda, you would tell me, wouldn't you?'

I shifted uneasily. 'I don't know, David. I'm engaged to you. I shall go through with it. What on earth good would it do if I said, look, I've fallen in love with someone else?'

'I wouldn't hold you,' he said, quietly.

My eyes widened with surprise. 'You'd let me go!'

'I have too much pride to hold you,' he said.

'Then you can't love me!' I stormed at him. 'After all you've said about it! You can't do! I know I wouldn't let anyone go–' and I broke off in confusion. I wasn't actively thinking of Nigel, but it struck me then that Nigel was always hazily there, at the back of my consciousness, as if he had somehow infused himself into that position, heaven knew when. I believe he had been there since I first met him, in the autumn, at home, and only his dinner parties and his outrageous proposal of marriage had made me realise it now.

'Wouldn't you?' David smiled. 'Perhaps women are different. I know I would never hold a woman in my arms, knowing she was perhaps imagining that I was someone else. Who could blame her, if her heart was with someone else.'

'You're torturing yourself,' I told him crossly.

'No, that's what you're doing to yourself. Linda, this friend of your aunt's–'

I couldn't stop the tell-tale colour from flooding my face. He watched me curiously, and went on.

'–have you spoken to him about Frances?'

In sheer relief, I said, quickly, 'Not yet, but I will do.'

He looked a little surprised. 'I thought perhaps as he was only a family friend, you might have brought that into the conversation fairly early on. You've seen him twice, haven't you?'

'I have,' I said, rather edgily.

'And you're going to see him again?'

'Every month,' I said firmly. 'It seems to have been arranged for me.'

'And it makes you angry,' he marvelled. 'Now why, I wonder? I didn't think from what you said about her, that your aunt was such a martinet. I thought you rather liked her.'

'I do. She's a dear.'

'Then why don't you tell her about me, and arrange a meeting – it's done, I believe, before the thing goes on too far. I should have thought you'd be the first to want to do the proper thing, Linda, with your up-bringing.'

'I've told you. I've told you again and again, David. It's my father who's the snag.'

'Oh, yes,' he agreed slowly. 'And he won't be away for a long time, will he, since he's only just come back from America.'

It was a question, and I had to answer it. Unwillingly I told David that he was going again soon, and that Aunt Berenice had told me to come down whenever I liked. I had to tell him because I had been thinking of seeing Aunt Berenice soon, to talk to her about Nigel. I could hardly go home again without telling David where I was going.

'It'll be the next weekend I'm free, I expect,' I said.

'Am I going with you, Linda?'

I didn't answer. It was all so very difficult. I had in mind that I would sound Aunt Berenice, to see if she really minded whom I married, because the whole thing raised rather a nice point. If her desire was just to see me happy, and I made her see that David was just the person to do that, then I didn't see how she could stand in my way. If, however, she had set her heart on my being Nigel's wife, that was rather different. Of course, I could do as I liked, but I had come to realise that I needed Aunt Berenice behind me. I hadn't so many people who were fond of me, that I could bear to throw over any. If I had been head over heels in love with David, I suppose it would have been different. I would have just gone ahead, and probably cut off from Marleigh Park anyway. I could never hope to keep the two different worlds going, as David's wife. I might not even want to.

'No, I see I am not going with you, my dear,' he smiled.

'David, you don't understand,' I began,

but he made a movement as if to brush the whole thing aside.

'Linda, listen. I've been given the opportunity of going out to Saudi Arabia as special correspondent. It's the chance I've waited for. It's not only a good job, but I've been wanting to do a book with that sort of background, and it will give me that chance without the expense of travelling. I'm going to take it.'

I gaped at him. 'When?'

'The job starts at the end of this week.'

'But you never said so before!'

'I've had very little time. I was actually on the point of turning it down, because it meant that I wouldn't see you for six months, probably more. Now I'm not sure. I think it might be a good plan if we didn't see each other for that period. You can make up your mind.'

He looked sombrely at me, while I took it in. Once before I had thought he was away, and the press of life was such that I hadn't even noticed his absence. Would it be like this now? But six months was a very much longer time.

'Don't mind, Linda, if you have to tell me it's all off when I come back,' he said. 'You see, I may be in love with you, but I'm not going to be any woman's doormat. I can do without you, if you've nothing at all to offer me.'

I tried to think of something to say, but I couldn't. It was in the nature of Nigel's shock tactics, and that wasn't like David. I thought at the time that he was probably trying out shock tactics on himself, too. Rushing himself into this thing, because he couldn't think of any other way out for either of us.

'If you feel you really want to go on with it,' David went on, 'then of course, there won't be much more time before you finish your training, and we can be married next winter.'

I said yes, faintly, and tried to pierce the veil of unreality, to see myself standing in bridal white at some small church altar, becoming David's wife, surrounded by David's family, and perhaps a few of our student nurses, the ones who had been closest to Frances and myself during our training. But I couldn't think of a clear picture. Unbidden came a picture, instead of Marleigh church, with Aunt Berenice and her friends, and Nigel and his old mother, and quite a different background altogether. A reception at the Park, and flying to Bermuda or Italy for a honeymoon.

I went back to the hospital soon after that. My head was aching, and I wished I had stayed in and studied that evening. Frances was lying flat on her bed, staring at the ceiling, and hardly bothered to look round at me.

'How did you get on with all that stuff?' I asked her, pointing to a tumbled pile of books and notepads on the floor by her bed.

'Might as well not have bothered. Can't concentrate,' she answered. 'Been lying here most of the time thinking about – oh, you know what. I just can't fix my mind on work.'

I decided that the next time I went to dinner with Nigel, I would tackle him about doing something for Frances and her Gordon. But I need not have bothered, as it happened.

Three mornings later, she came to me with a folded newspaper, and a delirious look on her face.

'Linda, look! It's awful to feel like this about someone dying, but honestly–' and she shoved it at me.

I didn't take it in at first, because the surname was unfamiliar, but before I could gather my wits, Frances had translated.

'It's Gordon's old aunt. She snuffed out last night. Don't you see? He's free now!'

Chapter Thirteen

If I had ever had any doubts about the feelings of Gordon Evans for Frances, they soon vanished. He had inherited everything from his aunt, and since the uncle with whom he lived had never been anything more than a hanger-on, he and Frances arranged to be married in a matter of eight weeks.

I quite thought that David would again put off his going abroad, at least to stay for her wedding, but he didn't. He went at the end of that week, as he had told me he would, and he didn't even see me again before he went.

'Have you two had a row again?' Frances asked me bluntly. She was dreadfully upset about David's not being at her wedding, and I think she was inclined to blame it on to me.

'No. We just hate this, that's all, and we're neither of us much good at goodbyes,' I said, rather evasively.

That weekend I went down to Marleigh Park. It was better than staying in town, and inevitably being invited to Frances's home. The position would be reversed now, I saw, and I had no stomach for having to sit there and discuss her wedding plans, with David not there. I couldn't decide whether I was being very arbitrary, or whether some feeling for him was beginning to stir.

I telegraphed to Aunt Berenice, to say that I was coming. She liked some sort of notice, and I didn't want to break in on any of her weekend parties. She telegraphed back at once to say that I would make an odd number, so she was inviting Nigel Armstrong as well.

I was disappointed. I had hoped that she wouldn't be having guests that weekend. I wanted to talk to her, in an unflurried atmosphere. She loved visitors, and never liked family discussions while guests were in the house.

Nigel, inevitably, got in touch with me and announced that he would run down in the car, and I couldn't slide out of that, either. I packed a few things, and wondered what this weekend would hold for me. At least it would keep David's departure out of my mind.

Frances stared speculatively as I put on the magnificent new dinner dress of shot grey silk. 'Isn't it a funny thing,' she said. 'I never thought I'd be having clothes like that, but I shall, shan't I?'

'Yes. And Bordenmere. Don't forget that.'

Bordenmere was the estate of Gordon's old aunt, a grim old Victorian mansion with great draughty rooms, and dreary grounds surrounding it, behind high walls. I'd never been in it, but I'd seen pictures of it, and heard our neighbours talking of it. It wasn't very near Marleigh Park, thank heavens, but near enough to cause the question in the eye of Frances. She was wondering, I knew, when I would suggest taking her down to Marleigh with me, to meet my aunt, now that things were so different.

'Linda, you'll have to help me run it,' Frances said, suddenly. 'You know about those things, and I haven't an idea. Honestly, I'm scared to death! I just never thought of that angle, when I was just in love with Gordon. It all seemed so remote. I never even thought of what it would be like if his old aunt relented and just invited me down to her rotten old place. But to have to run it, live there, know all those stiff-necked county people – Linda, you will help me won't you?'

'If I can,' I said, grinning ruefully. 'But don't forget I haven't had any experience of running anything. I just floated around and had a good time, and left everything to other people.'

'Yes, but it's your background. You'd know about it without consciously thinking of it,' she told me.

That flicked me on the raw, and made me think of Nigel and his proposal again, and the old anger surged up, so that all the way down to Marleigh in the car, I could hardly be civil to him.

It seemed to me that I was like a thoroughbred mare, who had been looked over, and purchased at great cost, both for her utilitarian qualities, and also for her good looks and nice nature. I hated it.

There were six other guests in the house, and I knew them all. This was the first time that Aunt Berenice had done anything to draw me back into the County after that unfortunate affair. She had insisted that people's memories were short, especially if there was an interesting wedding being arranged, and I found that that was so.

They were, for the most part, people near my aunt's age. Taking it by and large, they all had little liking for my father, but of course, he was their neighbour, and an excellent one, and he was also a very good bridge player, so they didn't let personal feelings come into the thing. But I daresay they were all rather pleased that he wasn't there on this occasion.

Aunt Berenice said to them all, 'You remember Linda, my little niece who decided to do something useful?' and it struck me that she had never really liked my becoming a nurse at all. She probably thought it was about equal to becoming a housemaid.

After dinner that first evening, the three wives were very nice to me, while Aunt Berenice talked delicately around the subject of Nigel, and what a sweet person he was. It was no secret to them all, I realised.

When the gentlemen came in, Nigel was very sweet and attentive to me, and I had the curious feeling of being already engaged to him, and that David didn't really exist.

We rode together next morning. The air was clear and frosty and my old riding kit (which I had left behind at Marleigh all the months I had been at the hospital) still fitted me well enough. I felt on top of the world, and again I marvelled at the beauty of the district and wondered why I didn't miss it more than I did. There were deep wooded valleys, and little low hills covered with sweet short turf that the horses loved. There was a scent of moss, and ferny hollows, and pine needles, and the tang of nearby farms.

We rode in silence for some time, and then Nigel said we would dismount. It was at the top of a rise. Tall pines thinned out and there was a magnificent view over the valleys, and the mist which hung over the tops of distant pines was a blue-ish grey in the early morning light. Over where the sun was rising, it was a mauvish pink, and all the colours intermingled below the skyline and became blurred and utterly beautiful.

Nigel came and stood close beside me,

looking at it.

'Does all this mean a great deal to you, Linda?'

'Enough,' I admitted. 'But I like London, too.'

He nodded, as if satisfied.

'Do you like me?' he asked suddenly.

The look he turned on me forced me to be honest.

'I don't think I quite know. At first, during that week we had together here, I thought I liked you very much.'

'And now you're not sure?'

'Now I'm not sure,' I murmured.

'I think I'd rather you felt almost any other emotion for me than just liking,' he told me with a smile. 'I want something much stronger from you.'

And then I think I realised that he wasn't the cold self-contained person I had imagined, at all. He certainly had a tremendous restraint on himself, and he probably was quite cool towards everyone else, but I think he believed he had to feel something much stronger for me, because of the role he wanted me to assume. Or perhaps he was forced against himself to feel something stronger. I don't know. I caught a flick of some very deep emotion in his eyes in that moment, and I was disturbed.

'Are you going to take very much longer to make up your mind?' he asked, in a conversational tone which contrasted oddly with that look.

My heart started to beat in an odd sort of way, as if I were being forced into this thing by some power beyond me. I knew I didn't have to go on with it. It would take a lot of courage to say outright that there was someone else, especially when Nigel would want to know who it was. I had the uncomfortable feeling that he would feel affronted, consider David a very social inferior and that it mattered a great deal more than if I had said I was going to marry another surgeon, for instance. But it wasn't only that. It was as if the forcing power were part of myself.

I tried to argue myself out of it, standing there. To marry Nigel meant asking David to release me (which he had said he would do, and therefore created no great difficulty) but it also meant telling Frances, too, and that would be most unpleasant. It would mean that I'd have to keep in the same circle of people as these at Marleigh now, and to know that even if they didn't mention that old affair, they were thinking of it all the time, and wondering where Alan was, and if he would come forward and make a nuisance of himself again. Moreover, they would always be waiting, expectant, to see me get mixed up in something of the sort, because in their hearts they believed what my father believed, that no one knew what was in my blood, and up till now nothing very good had come out of my antecedents.

And yet the urge was still there inside me, hammering at me. So that I felt I was torn into two; common sense saying no, no, no! and all the time my heart clamouring an insistent every-mounting yes.

'Is it such a very big problem?' Nigel asked, in a low, almost teasing voice.

I could hardly make myself speak, because I wasn't at all sure of my voice. At last I said,

'It seems such a business arrangement. I think I would have to marry for love.'

As I said it, it sounded all wrong. As if 'love' were something not to be mentioned. I recalled that the marriages of those in our circle at Marleigh were all more or less arranged, and pronounced suitable or un-suitable. No one ever mentioned that the couple were in love. They looked, at the altar, radiant, or merely satisfied. The way Nigel looked at me, rather bore me out. I had been guilty of not very good taste. An up-surge of the now familiar feeling of anger caught me then, and I nearly burst out with a remark to the effect that since I was no one, how could he expect me to take any other kind of view of marriage, but caution held my tongue. I didn't know whether Nigel knew about me, or whether Aunt Berenice had any intention of his knowing.

That I must find out, and very soon. But if she hadn't any intention of his knowing that I wasn't a Fane, then I could rely on all her friends to keep the secret.

'That's the way I feel about it,' I said, instead, and rather breathlessly. 'And I'm not sure if–'

'Aren't you?' he breathed, and with an expert economy of movement, he pulled me into his arms and kissed me.

I had been kissed a great deal, both by Alan and by David, but neither could produce anything comparable with this. I couldn't explain it, either. I had the sinking feeling that it was something I contributed to it myself. It wasn't excitement, as with Alan. It wasn't the saddening thing, as with David, when I felt I was trying to put something in my effort to match his own devoted brand of kiss, and there just wasn't anything there for me to put into it. No, this was something quite different, and oddly reminded me, in a flashing thought across my emotions, of Frances and her agonised look when she was anxious about Gordon, and of the painful happiness when she wasn't anxious about him. It was a drowning sensation, like fighting for your existence in a tide you thought you could manage. It was like trying to control a runaway horse, and not quite sure if you would succeed. There was a roaring in my ears and I couldn't open my eyes, and there was despair mixed with elation.

Nigel wasn't at all his usual calm self, either. He let me go at last, and I couldn't meet the stormy look in his eyes. And then I was conscious of his calling up everything he had, to subdue that onslaught of turbulence within him. If I thought he was going to tell me he loved me, I was bitterly disappointed.

All he said was, as he slowly put me away from him, 'I think that rather settles it, don't you? I'll see your aunt, at the first opportunity, and leave her to announce it.'

He took my arm, and said, looking at my horse, 'I think we'll get back now,' and I felt he was rather annoyed with himself because he sounded a little breathless as he spoke.

Before Aunt Berenice announced the engagement to her guests on the Sunday evening, she saw me alone in her room.

'Well, my dear, you've pleased me very much,' she said.

'Aren't you going to ask me if I love him?' I asked her, very much daring, and yet wanting so badly to know.

'I don't think so,' she said, calmly.

'That doesn't come into it?' I pressed.

'It's a very suitable match,' she said, firmly.

'But supposing it doesn't work out afterwards?' I insisted.

'You both get on well together, and that's all that matters for the present. The thing is the match itself, not what happens afterwards. But there is one thing I must impress on you, Linda. Nigel comes from a very good family. He must, of course, know nothing about your ... origins.'

'You mean he doesn't know I'm a foundling?'

She winced under that hated word.

'Your adoption was made legal. You legally took the name of Fane at birth. Everything is made out in that name. It's most imperative that he shouldn't know. If, of course, he finds out afterwards–'

'But that isn't honest!' I flared.

'Neither was the unfortunate business in which you dabbled, my dear,' she reminded me, and under her sweetness was a thin streak of coldness that I hadn't seen before, and which was a warning. I was inclined to forget that she was my father's sister, and not my mother's.

'You believe I was in it as much as Alan, then,' I said rather reproachfully, but she ignored that.

'What is more to the point, is that the late Mrs Fane's estate was bequeathed to you on your making a *suitable* marriage.'

I took quite some time to take that in. I knew little or nothing of what Mother had been worth, and I had cared even less where it went.

'Would it have come to me, whoever I married?' I wanted to know. 'I mean who are the Trustees?'

'The solicitors, I'm afraid,' she said, and she wasn't very pleased. I saw that she felt she ought to have been one, and her brother the other.

'Where would it have gone, if I hadn't made what the Trustees considered a "suitable" marriage?'

'Well, you *are* making a suitable marriage,' she said.

'But if I married someone they didn't approve of,' I insisted.

'The question simply doesn't arise,' she said.

I couldn't shift her, and I could see no real reason why I should dig in my heels and demand to see the documents. After all, as she said, my marriage to Nigel would be approved.

'So I'm an heiress,' I said, and it didn't sound real.

'But don't forget, not a word about your birth.'

I didn't like it, and I had other worries. I had still to write a rather awful letter to David, reminding him that he had promised to set me free, and that I was pleasing my aunt by this marriage. The only comforting thought I had was that he guessed already, and that was why he had said it, and also why he had gone away.

I spent most of the night, when I ought to have been sleeping, composing the thing, and then I couldn't sleep for wondering what I would say to Frances. Surely Nigel and I would be invited to her wedding, since Nigel was Gordon's superior, and I was Frances' best friend? But how would she feel about me, when she knew about David?

Nigel drove me back to Town the next day, and no one would have thought, to look at him, that he was the same person who kissed me up in the woods.

He talked chiefly about the hospital, and about the young woman called Elise Gladwin, who was slowly dying under his eyes. He had had several new and tricky cases since I'd gone off that ward, and he had a cool and calm way of viewing every one of them, like a schoolboy who knows he is good at maths, and simply clears the decks for action on the next problem. That's all they were, I felt, these women patients of his; tricky problems to tackle.

I wondered if all surgeons were the same, and whether Gordon Evans would be like that, too, or whether he had a little more feeling. After all, I had seen one of his private and personal notes to Frances, the one she had shown me at Christmas, and that didn't suggest to me that he was cold like Nigel.

At the first opportunity, I told her about the whole thing.

It had to come sooner or later, and I felt it was better to tell her while she was actually in hospital with me, than to wait until I had to meet her socially, in case she altered, as she was rather bound to. After all, I would still be, as far as she was concerned, merely a student nurse, while she would be the wife of an up and coming young houseman.

She didn't seem as surprised as I thought she would be. She said she had seen it coming, and didn't hesitate to tell me how rotten she thought I was.

'Our David was the biggest fool, not to drop you when he could have.'

'I haven't made any secret of my feelings for him, and anyway, before he went away, he insisted that I should tell him if I wanted to be free.'

'And you've taken him up on that!'

'Naturally. There's no point in making him more unhappy by trying to deceive him. He'd find out, anyway.'

'Are you leaving him to find out, or are you writing to him?' she asked scathingly.

'I'm writing to him – I posted a letter last night,' I said, angrily, 'and anyway, I didn't have to tell you all this, Frances!'

'I don't know why you did,' she said, coldly.

I shrugged.

'In the ordinary way I wouldn't be seeing you again, but it isn't so easy, is it, since Gordon and Nigel–?'

She hadn't thought of that, and it didn't please her very much.

'Does Gordon know about my having been engaged to David?' I asked suddenly, thinking with dismay that I had forgotten that angle.

'Of course. Haven't you told Nigel Armstrong about my brother?'

'Naturally not.'

'I should have thought it would be the only decent thing to do. Suppose he finds out?'

'He can only find out from you or Gordon Evans.'

'Oh, we won't say anything,' she said, rather contemptuously.

'Aren't you going to hope that I'll be very happy?' I smiled.

'I don't think I care a damn,' she said, and left me.

Chapter Fourteen

Frances was married in mid-March. It was a strange feeling, seeing only pictures of her wedding, after the deep friendship we had had in the hospital.

Neither Nigel nor I attended. Nigel absolutely refused to. He was so angry with Gordon for marrying one of the nurses. He told me all about it, and how he considered that Gordon had jettisoned all his chances for a brilliant future.

'I don't quite see,' I felt bound to object. 'I know her. She's a very nice type.'

'That's just your insane loyalty, Linda. The whole thing's wrong.'

'But you're marrying a nurse, too,' I objected smilingly.

'I'm marrying a Fane of Marleigh,' he corrected me, and he looked so coldly at me that I was tempted to wonder if he really knew the truth.

'That sounds medieval,' I said, trying not to laugh.

'Don't be flippant about your family, Linda. Birth and breeding mean a great deal to me. Everything, in fact.'

'Wouldn't you have married me if I hadn't

been Linda Fane?' I asked him.

'I do so dislike hypothetical questions,' he said, testily. 'Please don't ask me any more, Linda. They make me very angry. There are quite enough relevant questions to be answered, without wasting time and dissipating energy by bothering about situations that have not happened nor are they ever likely to.'

'Oh,' I said, feeling crushed and very small and young.

Nevertheless, Frances made a very beautiful bride, and looked quite poised and confident. Afterwards, I discovered with some amusement, that Gordon's uncle, with whom he lived, had found an impoverished gentlewoman to groom Frances, and be her maid and companion. I didn't think there were any left, nor did I think Frances would ever consent to have one, but I was wrong.

Oddly enough, I heard about it from David's father.

Much to my embarrassment, I ran into him one day when I was out for a couple of hours. We both happened to be looking in the same bookshop. I flushed, and would have turned away and walked on, but he took my arm, and said he would buy me a coffee.

As he sat facing me in the little teashop down the side street, I searched his face for any condemnation, but there wasn't any there.

'Aren't you angry with me, at all?' I asked.

'I don't think so,' he said, quietly.

'Not even about David?'

'Haven't you made your mind up, even now, Linda?' he asked me.

'Oh, yes. Yes I have. But I thought you'd be the last to – well, I was more or less taken into the family, wasn't I?'

'We may not keep a code of rules, as your people do, my dear, and that may be your people's misfortune. We liked you, for what you were. The fact that you couldn't bring yourself to be our David's wife, doesn't mean to say that we don't like you any more. I'm glad, for one, that you were honest about it. It would have meant a lot of unhappiness for you both, I'm sure, if you'd just gone ahead, determined to stick to your bargain. No one can force the heart to do what one wishes.'

'I'm glad you feel like that,' I said.

He watched me thoughtfully.

'And does David feel like that?' I asked him.

'Yes, I think so. He didn't say much. Didn't he write and wish you happiness?'

I shook my head. 'Neither did Frances. We fell out about it. She thinks I'm a contemptuous piece of work.'

He smiled faintly, 'Frances is young, and rather headstrong. Perhaps she'll understand what you did when she's been in her new life a little longer.'

'But if you understand, why doesn't she? How does David's mother feel about it?'

'She's very sorry about you, my dear. She thinks you'd have been happier with us than with Mr Armstrong. It isn't any of our business, but from what Frances has told us about him, he doesn't sound the type– Well, well, that isn't for me to say, and no doubt you know best. You know him better than we do.'

'Why do you feel like that?' I asked curiously, but he wouldn't say any more about it.

'I want you to promise me something, Linda.'

'If I can,' I said carefully. 'I might not feel I can, mind.'

'I want you to feel that if you're in trouble, and you can't go to your fine friends and relations, you can come to us.'

It was such an unexpected thing to say, that it brought a lump into my throat.

'That's a very kind thing to say,' I managed at last. 'But why? Why did you say it? Why should you think–?'

'Oh, I don't know,' he said, 'things come along, and one needs a place to go, someone to turn to. Someone you can let your back hair down to, and know it doesn't matter.'

'It … might be a very hard thing to do, the way I've treated David,' I ventured.

'No,' he smiled, shaking his head. 'I think one day you'll find it instinctive.'

'But why? I'm Linda Fane. I'm going to marry Nigel Armstrong and have a Town house and an estate in–'

He shook his head.

'I know lass. Don't make an inventory of material things. I wasn't thinking of all that. I was thinking, and I often have, that if you hadn't told us of that fine home of yours, and your rich friends and relatives, I'd say that you were quite alone in the world, and pretty unhappy and lonely with it. Yes, I'd say that you needed a family like us to turn to.'

'I wish I'd have come to Frances's wedding,' I said. 'I didn't want to meet you all. It didn't seem easy.'

'The trouble with you young people is that you don't give the older ones credit for understanding. If you'd only come to us and tell us things.'

I wondered if that was just to remind me of what he said to me once, that I was to come and confide in him, or whether he were deploring Frances and her marriage, of which she had told them practically nothing until she had to. He even gave no indication of whether he approved or disapproved of Gordon. He just never mentioned him.

On that note, my lack of confidence in the older people, he left me. I had no intention of going to see the family, of course. The Blakes, as far as I was concerned, were right out of my orbit altogether now, and so I forgot that meeting. If I could have only seen into the future, and caught a glimpse of the circumstances which would lead me to meet them again, I think even I would have quailed. As it was, I shrugged them off my shoulders, and went back to the hospital, thinking only about Nigel, and getting my S.R.N.

Soon after that, I went on night duty again, on the Men's Surgical. Most of the men were elderly, and no trouble at all, and very little of their sufferings penetrated, as the women's had.

I was sailing ahead towards my finals, and had a lot more confidence in the things I was doing. I liked Night Sister, and I got on well with the Night Staff Nurse. There were no haemorrhages, and there were no crises at all for the first three nights.

I had been shifted to the floor below, in the hostel, since Frances left. We were due for a move, anyway, with less senior people taking our places. I now had a room of my own, and it was very pleasant. I missed Frances at first, but it was rather nice to know that no matter what happened, there was no room mate to have to tell everything to.

I was thinking of Alan, and how difficult it

had been to keep Frances from finding out too much, when he suddenly sky-rocketed into my life again, by sending a note, by hand, to tell me to let him into the bathroom again that night.

I absolutely panicked. It was the most appalling bad luck to have happened to me. I couldn't get in touch with him to stop him, because I had no idea where to find him. I couldn't get to that particular bathroom, because having been moved down from that floor, I had no further right to be up there. Also, the bathroom below didn't have the fire escape running past it. Owing to the peculiar shape of the building, and the cramped space, the fire escape ran along a small runway and down the side of another part of the building, so I couldn't reach him from the bathroom on our floor. Quite apart from all this, I wouldn't be in the hostel at that time, being on night duty.

I examined mentally all the other nurses who had started at the same time as Frances and myself, to see if I could get any one of them to help me. But we hadn't been particularly friendly with them, owing to our own very close partnership, and so I could hardly hope in that direction. My only plan was to keep looking from the windows on that side of the building, to try and watch the fire escape, and then to dash over to the hostel, and up to that bathroom and quickly explain the situation to him, arranging a meeting at some other time. If I were caught, which wasn't very likely, I should have to think up some reason for being where I shouldn't be.

It would have been all right, if only Alan had arrived at a time when I was due for a meal, but he didn't. I had been back from my meal some forty minutes, when I thought I saw a dark shape on the fire escape. It moved, and I knew it was him, outlined black against the blur of light from the street beyond. I hoped and prayed that no one else would see him, and told my junior that I was just going to slip out to the penny-house.

The Men's Surgical was split into two small wards, and there were two of us, my junior and myself, and the Night Staff Nurse, in ours, the same number in the far one. Both the Staff Nurses were down at their meal at the time, and it would have been easy. Unfortunately for me, just as I had gone, a call came through to prepare an operation bed.

My junior rushed to the penny-house to find me, and couldn't, and for one brief and awful moment, no one was in the ward. My junior did the next best thing and dashed into the adjoining ward and told Nurse Benny, who had joined about the same time as Frances and myself, and reckoned herself one of our bunch. She had had the room next but one to ours when we were on the floor above, and perhaps if Frances and I hadn't been such close friends, I would have been more friendly with Benny.

She covered up for me, and as it happened, the Staff Nurses came back just then, and the op- bed was prepared. But I had to face the music just the same.

I think if it hadn't been for Nigel straightening things out for me, my hospital career might have ended then. My story of having dashed back to the hostel for a hankie was feeble in the extreme. I should have made do with a length of gauze or something, not left my ward to a junior. But worse than that, one of the senior nurses had found me on that fatal upper floor, and swore she heard me talking to someone, in the bathroom. What she was doing up there, I couldn't imagine, but that didn't come into it.

It was a nasty patch, and even though it was smoothed over, it left a great big question-mark, both with Matron, and with Nigel.

Nigel was particularly annoyed about it all, because to him it seemed such a senseless thing to do, and it had forced him into using our engagement as a lever to get me off trouble with Matron. He didn't like having to do that, at all. His fiancée had to be blameless, and I had committed one of the most awful crimes possible – I had left my ward while I was virtually in charge. It might not have been so bad if the Staff Nurse had been on the ward at the time.

And then of course Nigel wanted to know why I had done it.

'I can't imagine what you were about!' he kept saying. 'You must have had a good reason for it!'

And when no explanation was forthcoming, he went back to the rumour that I had been heard talking to someone.

That I emphatically denied. I had to. But I did have many uneasy moments about that. I had been talking to Alan, and he hadn't bothered to lower his voice. Supposing that senior nurse had heard a man's voice answering me, or worse still had heard what Alan had said?

'I'm in a real spot, this time,' he had said, and absolutely refused to go, on the grounds that I was on duty and would talk to him another time. The sum he mentioned appalled me.

'Don't be a fool. Where have I got all that much money?' I asked him.

'You've fixed your engagement to this Armstrong bloke. Tap him for it.'

'And break up my engagement? That would be funny, wouldn't it?'

He had the sense to agree that that

wouldn't be a bright idea, but it didn't help me much, when he promptly produced another and better plan. 'Aunt Berenice. Lift your trousseau money off her. It's about time you started thinking about it.'

'And what would I settle my bills with?' I asked him tartly.

'Don't. Run 'em up, and settle 'em after you're married.'

He assumed his old threatening attitude again, and with a great deal more pungency. Now he could not only get me thrown out of hospital if he liked, but he could break up my marriage to Nigel.

If ever I was in a cleft stick, it was now.

I decided to tackle Aunt Berenice, if only to keep Alan quiet. But my father had come home unexpectedly, and so I couldn't go down there. I had to wait, and to think up some other plan.

Alan, it appeared, had got into real trouble this time. He had, during that prosperous period of a few months ago, been working with some new people he had come up against, and they were all doing very well. I didn't ask what the 'work' was, but knowing Alan, I guessed that that was a very dig-nified name to attach to his activities. Then, reading between the lines, I discovered that Alan had double-crossed one of his asso-ciates, and had to get out of the country again.

'You don't know what loyalty is, do you?' I asked him scathingly, as we sat in his newest flat drinking coffee which he had made over a portable stove. This place was completely shoddy. It didn't even smell clean, and he shared it with some other people who were out when he was in. I didn't like it at all.

'Look, I'm not asking for gifts, Linda, just a loan now and then, when I really need it. When I'm on top, I pay you back, now don't I?'

I admitted that he had done so, the last time, but that was no guarantee that he would keep on doing so.

'I need as much as I can get. Have you got any ice you can hock, just to help me out?'

'If you think you're going to get my engagement ring, you've got another think coming,' I said, indignantly and inelegantly. 'I have to wear the thing whenever I'm off duty.'

He insisted on examining Nigel's big diamond he had given me and appraised it. 'Nice work. Can't you say you lost it? Then when I can lay my hands on enough, you can get it out again, and tell your super-man you found it.'

'He hasn't the sort of nice mind to believe such a story,' I said, acidly. 'Besides, I don't care for the idea either.'

'Want that engagement broken up, Lin?'

'It wouldn't help you, in the long run,' I

reminded him.

I talked to Aunt Berenice on the telephone, on inspiration, and begged her to
advance me enough money out of my
expectations, to start a bank account, as I
found I needed so much extra money.
Surprisingly she did, but that money ran out
too quickly. To keep Alan away from the
hospital, I kept all on giving him cash, and
at last, I was penniless again.

'You fool, why didn't you take what I gave
you, and get out, if that's what you wanted?'
I asked him, desperately.

'It was never enough at one time, and by
the time I got any more out of you, the first
lot had gone. Get me a decent sum and then
I won't bother you.'

'Alan,' I said, in despair, 'why won't you
leave me alone? Why must you keep making
my life a misery?'

'But you're my favourite cousin!' He
chuckled. 'I'm so fond of you, I can't bear to
be very far from you. And come to think of
it, I don't show you enough affection.
Despite what you said about taxis, I think
we'll have to put that state of affairs right.'

By the time the summer came, life was
beginning to be a very great strain. I still
dined once a month with Nigel, but there
were times when I felt that he was still
worrying round that old subject, the unexplained mystery of the voice in the

upstairs bathroom. He was like a dog worrying at a rat-hole. He'd give every appearance of having forgotten about the unavailing struggle, and then he'd go back to it for a last sniff.

I went down to Marleigh one weekend in June. I had actually a week off, but I didn't spend it all there. Part of it I had promised to Frances, who had made it up with me. Gordon Evans was still as coldly polite as he had ever been. I think he felt as furious about my engagement to Nigel, as Nigel did about his marriage to Frances. The two men rarely spoke outside of hospital, and it must have made their daily association trying, but Gordon felt, I think, that Nigel ought to have at least known about my previous engagement to his brother-in-law.

Aunt Berenice was very pleased to see me, until I broached the topic of money again, and that seemed to be a point that was going to be extremely difficult.

'But Linda, dear, I don't think I quite understand. You've had so much money, and you've never spent so much before, since you've been at the hospital, to my knowledge.'

'I wasn't engaged to Nigel then,' I smiled.

'Are you buying so many new clothes, then?'

'Oh, I need it in hosts of ways,' I said, evasively.

'Three hundred pounds?' she asked.

I hadn't expected her to keep so close an eye on the money I had had. It struck me as being rather absurd, since I was going to have so much of my own one day.

'Aunt Berenice, I've had to practise poverty, all this time in hospital, because it looked as if it would be the way I'd always have to live. But it was frightfully difficult, worrying at times. Now that you tell me I'm to have a lot of money of my own, why should I keep up that old anxiety of being careful? What does it matter how much I spend? It's going to be mine, isn't it?'

'You haven't married Nigel yet,' she said.

'But I'm going to. Have you any reason to think I shan't?'

'Nigel has been rather uneasy about something which appeared to have happened when you were on night duty,' she said slowly.

'He told you so?' I gasped.

'He called, two weekends ago, when he was passing. He was staying at Colonel Tilburn's for the weekend, and he felt he would like to talk to me about it.'

'But he didn't tell me he'd seen you!'

'Have you seen him since then?'

'On the wards. Not to talk to privately,' I confessed.

'Then he hasn't had a chance to tell you. But I've no doubt he will tell you. He isn't in the habit of being secretive.'

'Neither am I,' I flared.

'I think you are, or you'd tell me what you want all this money for.'

'But I have told you! Besides, I want to get my trousseau together.'

'Well, you don't need money for that, child. I was going to help you do that myself, but there's plenty of time. Nigel tells me that you're going to pass your final examinations first, before you are married.'

I had never found Aunt Berenice inflexible like this before. I prowled round the room, and a thought struck me that hadn't occurred to me before.

'Does my father know about my engagement?'

'He does.'

'What does he – what will he–?'

'You're wondering how his hostility will appeal to Nigel, in view of our keeping the past discreetly veiled? Don't worry. Your father will never let the family down at a time like this. He'll give you away, as he would have done in happier times. And he'll give you the wedding gift that poor Elizabeth would have wanted. He knew how much you meant to her.'

'I think he's a hypocrite!' I flung at her.

'Linda, I've noticed it before dear – your manners have deteriorated since you left Marleigh. Be careful. Nigel won't like that!'

'And Mother wouldn't have liked Father pretending to be nice to me when all the time he hated me!'

Characteristically, she made no answer to that.

Instead, she said, 'Have you seen Alan lately?'

It caught me on the raw.

'Why did you ask me that, Aunt Berenice?'

'Well, have you?'

'No,' I said, lying desperately. If I'd admitted I had, she would have wanted to know more, and more.

'Oh, that's splendid. It occurred to me that Alan might be getting this money from you.'

'You think I'd give him money?' I gasped.

'I'm pretty sure you would, if you thought he could do any real damage to your hospital career.'

'Well, would you blame me, Aunt Berenice?'

'Certainly I'd blame you,' she said, hardily. 'I wouldn't give you a penny if I thought that was where it was going.'

'What would you do, if you were me, and you thought there was a possibility of his seeing that Matron knew certain things?'

'How could he?'

'Alan might even stoop to sending an anonymous letter. He'd know I couldn't deny anything, and there's no smoke without fire.'

'My dear child, do you think anyone would believe a single thing against one of us? You're still a Fane, you know!'

'Aunt Berenice, I don't think Matron would care if I were the Queen of Sheba. If I couldn't assure her that I'd had a perfectly blameless life, she wouldn't want me to be one of her nurses. She's like that. She says that if you haven't a spotless character, you aren't any good for Bardmore's. I can't say that I blame her.'

'What makes you so sure that Alan would go to the trouble of getting you removed from your hospital?'

'He's spiteful. If he couldn't–'

'–couldn't what?' she purred.

'If he felt like it, he'd do even that to hurt me,' I finished lamely. I was going to say, if he couldn't get as much money as he wanted, and I'm pretty sure she knew that.

'No, Alan isn't spiteful. He's weak. He's money mad. If he can't get it, by fair means, he doesn't mind what means he goes to, so long as he doesn't hurt himself. But if he found there was no means of getting money from that particular source, I doubt if he'd do harm there. I've refused him money, and he hasn't tried to injure me. He just grinned good-naturedly, and said, all right, I quite understand. He didn't like being refused, but he's no fool. If he ever pesters you,

219

child, just call his bluff. He won't go to your Matron.'

'I wish I could be sure of that,' I muttered.

'I wish I could be sure that you were telling me the truth,' she countered, and wrote me the cheque I had been asking for.

Chapter Fifteen

I was glad to get away from Marleigh Park. I travelled across country to Frances's place and wondered what sort of rest I would get there. Frances was staying at Bordenmere for the summer, and Gordon drove himself down each evening from Town. She seemed quite happy, and not nearly so involved with difficulties as I had expected, chiefly owing to the untiring efforts of Mrs de Witt, her companion. Mrs de Witt arranged everything, and there was an excellent staff there, personally trained by Gordon's great-aunt, who was a martinet for precision and efficiency. I thought Frances was very lucky, and realised that since she wasn't used to such a background, she didn't know just how lucky she was.

We managed to get a little heart-to-heart talk one evening, and then she asked me straight out about Alan, and how he fitted into the new Nigel-dominated arrangements.

'What d'you mean ... fit in?' I asked.

'Well, does Nigel know about him?'

'Don't be a mutt. Of course he doesn't,' I said, crossly.

'He soon will,' she prophesied.

I felt my heart turn over. I had been so confident in managing Alan myself, so hopeful that if I could get enough money, he would go right out of the country, or leave me alone, that I hadn't thought of him ever going to Nigel.

Frances said, 'I never thought you'd let yourself in for his nonsense,' and smiled at the delicate wording of that sentence. Before Mrs de Witt's time, Frances would have come out bluntly with the very ugly word which Alan's 'nonsense' really merited. 'Fancy keeping on coughing up money, just when he asks for it!'

'It's because I know him so well. I'm so used to him,' I said, wonderingly. 'If it had been a stranger, anyone else, in fact, I'd have got mad and gone straight to the police, and to the devil with the consequences. But not with Alan. Not with someone in your own family. Alan's stayed in our house, ate there, danced there, practically lived there at one time.'

'Yes, I see your point. I'm not blaming you. I'm surprised that you've put up with it so long, Linda.'

A little silence fell between us, which she at last broke.

'It's so funny. It seemed so right and proper that you should be engaged to our David, and practically in our family. I just can't see you married to Nigel Armstrong. I can't see the set-up – you sitting like a good little wife, listening to that stuffed-shirt – oh, sorry, I shouldn't be rude about people I know!'

'Is that what Mrs de Witt says?' I grinned. Oddly I didn't mind her saying things about Nigel, especially when, despite everything, I sometimes found myself thinking just the same thing.

'Yes. It's true, especially as you're so keen on Nigel.'

I flushed hotly. 'Who says I am? I'm not really keen on anyone!'

She looked rather sorry for me, I thought. 'Mind you're not getting up a nice protective pose, about all that, Linda. You're not going to be any more immune from falling in love than anyone else. I think you've fallen pretty badly for Nigel Armstrong.'

'Oh, he certainly fascinates me, but I don't think–'

'You can't run away from deep feelings, you know,' she told me, with very rare wisdom, for her. 'You're bound to get hurt at some time or other. Everyone seems to. It's life, I suppose. But it's going to be a jolly sight harder if you keep on running away from it all. Much easier if you face up to it, because in a way it shortens the discomfort, in terms of time.'

'I've taken enough knocks from Fate,' I said, angrily, 'and I know that's something one can't help. But getting hurt from being stupid enough to fall in love, no, that's something that one can avoid, and I mean to, if I can.'

'I don't think one can avoid it, even if one wants to,' Frances said. 'Oh, don't mind me knowing, and talking like this, Linda. I've been through it. I know all the signs, and I would say you'd got it pretty badly. It's been coming on a long time, too. I used to think it was for our David, and then I realised it wasn't, and I couldn't think who it was. I didn't know what to think, when I found out. It was all so improbable, until I recalled that your aunt knew Nigel, and that you'd most likely fall for someone in your own world, anyway.'

She never ventured on the subject of whether Nigel cared for me. There wasn't much time, anyway. Once Gordon was in the house, we had a chilly dinner and chillier bridge afterwards. People, neighbours mostly, drifted in (invited, no doubt, by Mrs de Witt), and cool and well-planned evenings were the rule. I wondered how long Frances was going to exist in that de Witt-ish atmosphere, but apparently she neither minded nor liked them particularly. It was enough for her that Gordon was there, and that he was happy. Sometimes I caught a look pass between them, when they were far enough away from anyone else, and it was enough to assure me that they were still very much in love.

On the whole it was a relief to go back to the hospital. The weather was lowering, hot and sticky, with storms imminent. It was next to impossible to stay in and study, in my free time, and yet I knew I dare not go out now, and risk wastage of precious hours. The time was running out, and I had dissipated a lot of energy (as Nigel would put it) in worry about things which had nothing to do with my career and exams.

One evening, unable to bear the heat and oppressiveness any longer, I went out of the hospital, and down to the river. It was a little cooler there, and I walked along the embankment, looking down at the water, which always seemed to be grey, and thinking of that wet, deserted morning I spent there with David. I forgot that he was expected back in July, and I almost felt that I was looking at a ghost, leaning over the stone parapet. This illusion was helped by his just standing there, looking at me with such a sorrowful look in his dark eyes.

'David!' I breathed, and held the stone-work for support.

'Hello, Linda,' he said, in a low voice, and it seemed with an effort he turned, lifted his hat, and shook hands with me.

'Was it such a shock, seeing me, or didn't you know I'd come back?' he said.

He looked vaguely unfamiliar, and I realised he was very tanned. His skin had always been darkish, not the pale olive that was the special beauty of Frances. There was, too, an unfamiliar air about him which I could only put down to the extra confidence he had gathered, no doubt from his travels and his job. I felt that he was a complete stranger, and I didn't like the feeling.

'I don't know,' I said.

'I came here to rustle up a few ghosts, but you look as if you'd seen one,' and he smiled, a faint remote smile that I hadn't seen before. 'How are you?'

He glanced at my left hand, where Nigel's ring was, and I saw him lift his eyebrows.

'It's a little different, I'm afraid, being engaged to one of the hospital honoraries,' I told him.

'How?' he wanted to know. 'You wouldn't wear my ring,' he reminded me.

'I have to do as I'm told.'

'Really, Linda? But I thought you were doing as you wanted. Aren't you happy?'

'I suppose so.'

'That doesn't sound very good. Didn't it work out, my dear?'

I shrugged my shoulders. I hated inquisitions, and I didn't like David's common sense being brought on to a problem. I never had.

'Oh, I don't know. I feel as if I'm two people, and one of them is pushing me into all sorts of situations.'

'But you *are* in love with the fellow?' he probed.

'Yes. At least, Frances says I am,' I grinned.

'I heard you two had made it up. I'm glad of that,' he said. Then, thinking, 'How long have you got? Wouldn't you like to come home and see them all? They'd love it, you know.'

'Oh, no. I don't think so,' I said, hurriedly. Nothing was further from what I needed, just then.

He looked hurt. 'Oh, I forgot. You're probably waiting to meet Torringfield. I'll leave you, then.'

'No. No, I'm not! Don't go, David.'

He seemed surprised at that, and I was rather surprised myself. I couldn't have said why I had prevented him from leaving me. It was more, I suppose, that I didn't want to be alone just then.

'Tell me about your work. Was this job all you had hoped for? Did you start on the book?'

He smiled, and stood talking to me for some little time, until at least even I knew I had to call a halt to it. We were both behaving like a pair of fools, chasing shadows, trying to call up memories, when we had no business to. He was dreaming over the ghosts of other days when I had met him in my free hours and we had talked like this. I was trying to pretend that I was not really unhappy over Nigel, or that I had really let David go. It just didn't make sense.

When I left him, with a solemn handshake, I wondered if I was being all sorts of a fool to be seen talking to other men, so near to the hospital. Since I had become engaged to Nigel I had become aware of an element in the hospital which must have been there all the time, but which didn't affect me when I was engaged to David. It was the underground jealousy and suspicion, for one of the nurses who had had the luck to become engaged to an honorary. That did happen, of course, but I sensed the feeling that I personally had entered the hospital half way there, since it now seemed generally known that I had a wealthy home and a better background than most of the others.

I felt a prick of misgiving as I recalled the face of the Staff Nurse who had caught me on the upper floor of the hostel. She was a hard-bitten, hard-working, thoroughly efficient, but plain and hopelessly spinster-type woman. No one ever believed she would ever marry, and she had a deep-rooted contempt for those girls who came into the hospital, embarked on a course of training, and became engaged long before they were half through it.

I wondered whether she had really heard Alan's voice that night, and whether she had made it her business to tell Matron. If she had heard anything he had said, then of course, trouble for me was not yet over. It was purely an instinctive feeling, that. So far as I could tell, Nigel had smoothed things out for me, because he naturally had a prior interest in the matter. But it behoved me to step carefully, and how could I, with Alan always at my heels?

I had the money ready to give him, and that was an anxiety. I had it in cash, in a pocket belt beneath my uniform, so that if he sent one of those flying notes of his, I wouldn't have to worry about dashing to the bank, or having to tell him that he must wait till the bank opened the next day. In the note with the money, I had said, and underlined it, 'This is the last time.' I debated the wisdom of putting anything into writing, but as I hadn't signed it, I didn't see that it could possibly matter. But it was necessary to give the sentiment in black and white, for Alan rarely listened to anything I said, and if he did, he merely laughed at me.

The next morning, I had a letter from him. It came through the post, and it had no address on it. Here he always had me. I could never get in touch with him. The flat he had had a matter of weeks ago, was now a thing of the past. For all I knew, he had no address, and merely stayed for odd nights in various places. It didn't do to enquire too closely into his movements. But for me, the new worry was that he insisted in this present note that he was coming to see me that afternoon. I was to meet him outside. Just like that. The fact that I might be on duty (and I was) hadn't occurred to him.

I worried around how I could possibly get outside at three o'clock. It was the visiting hour. If I could only slip down and give him the package without being seen, but in broad daylight?

Finally I decided to take the gate porter into my confidence. He was a nice little man, a Cockney through and through, and he had often turned a blind eye when Frances and I had come in late at nights. I told him a tale about wanting to get a little package to my cousin, and she not being able to get out from her job, but that her young man was coming over, and would be waiting outside the gate. I described Alan as best I could, and having done up the cash and the note in a small cardboard box, and addressed it to 'Miss A Torringfield,' I left it with him and hoped for the best. He promised he would keep an eye open for anyone 'lurking-like,' and ask him if he was waiting for Nurse Fane.

We had a busy time that day. The honoraries went round with their bunches of students like a devoted bodyguard, and Sister walked beside them, crackling with importance, and besides being late in arriving, they stayed much too long and threw everything out, so that the visitors had almost arrived before we were ready. We had had a couple of casualties sent up for receiving from the operating theatre, and a haemorrhage flung in for luck. My head was aching by the time the first trickle of visitors was allowed in. They queued on the stairs, just like a bus-queue, with the same amount of packages and parcels, bunches of flowers, and air of submissive waiting.

I opened the ward door and jammed it with the wooden wedge, and got out first, before they stampeded me with the solid crush. And then to my horror, a man detached himself from the queue, and said, in a voice that carried everywhere:

'Oh, Nurse, I don't think I'm on the right floor. Can you direct me to–?'

I briskly walked over to him and went on walking, and he had to walk with me if he wanted an answer.

'What the blazes are you doing inside the hospital, Alan?' I muttered furiously.

'Why the blazes weren't you outside, as we arranged?' he returned.

'We didn't arrange it. If you'd asked me first, I'd have told you I couldn't manage it. I'm on duty. You can't stay here.'

'All you've got to do is give me what you promised me, and I'll go like a lamb,' he said.

We had got well away from the visitors now, and were at the end of the corridor. I was supposed to be in the kitchens cutting the patients' bread and butter and getting the trolleys ready.

'I left it in a parcel addressed to Miss Torringfield,' I muttered, in exasperation. 'The gate porter's got it, and he was to look out for you. You're supposed to be the man-friend of my girl cousin, and he was to give it to you.'

I was angry, and so was Alan. He looked alarmed as well.

'How much was there?' he stuttered.

'As much as you asked me for, and it's the last time.'

'Never mind that. Are you crazy, to leave all that much money lying about, in strange hands? Why didn't you make an excuse and get outside to see me. I bet you've done it other times, if you wanted to get out badly enough.'

'You'll get me thrown out of here yet,' I told him angrily. 'Go down to the–'

I had been going to say 'Gate Porter', but an interruption came, and it was luck for me that I got no further.

A familiar voice said, 'Is anything wrong, Nurse?' and I looked up to find Nigel there.

He never seemed to clear off out of the hospital with the same speed as the other honoraries. I had often wished he would, and never more earnestly than today.

I shrugged. 'This visitor lost the way, sir.'

Alan played up magnificently. 'I think I can find the ward I want now,' he said, smoothly. 'So sorry to have troubled you, Nurse,' and he walked sedately to the stairhead.

Nigel said, sharply, 'Was the fellow being a nuisance?'

'Just stupid, like most visitors,' I said. 'I must go back now, Nigel.'

He stopped me. 'You're off duty tonight, aren't you?'

I nodded.

'I'll pick you up at seven thirty,' and he walked off with a curious expression on his face.

It wasn't time for our monthly dinner, and as a matter of fact, I had been rather at a loose end, but would far rather have gone to the pictures on my own, than dined with Nigel after that little skirmish. He would come back to it again, I knew.

We dined at his London house, instead of an hotel. I wished we hadn't, the atmosphere was so frigid.

We had coffee served in the big, unfriendly lounge, and after he had lit a cigarette for me, and carefully fitted his own into his favourite holder, he said:

'Linda, did you know that man in the hospital today?'

I was completely surprised.

'I told you, Nigel, he was just a visitor.'

'I see. Only that?'

'What a funny thing to ask. It doesn't matter that I took a little trouble to help the man, does it? I wasn't neglecting my duty. I dashed straight back and got the trolleys ready on time.'

'I happened to go downstairs, on the fellow's heels.' Nigel said. 'He didn't go to any ward. He went down to the gate porter.'

He looked straight at me.

'Is it relevant?' I asked lightly.

'Yes, it is rather. He asked the gate porter for a package which Nurse Fane had left for him, and when he saw me behind him, he told the gate porter that it didn't matter, and cleared off.'

My face scorched. 'Nigel, do you know how all that sounds? You going down after a man who spoke to me in the corridor, and following him out to the porter? I don't like it.'

He looked rather coldly at me.

'Neither do I,' he agreed. 'But since you're not perfectly open with me, I have to tell

234

you that there's rather a lot of gossip going on in the hospital, about you. I don't like it, and it's got to stop. I'll go to any lengths to get to the bottom of it.'

'I hope this doesn't mean that you're going round after me for the rest of my life, getting to the bottom of every little thing I don't tell you!' I said, angrily.

'If we're to spend our lives together, Linda, it must be understood that there aren't any little things that you don't tell me. I have a responsible position, an important one, and I don't believe you've realised just what that means.'

'Oh, I have, Nigel,' I told him gravely.

'Then why do you do things that even the most ordinary little nurse would know was wrong. You in your position should be above reproach!'

'Aren't I?' I asked, quietly.

That surprised him. 'I'd hardly say you were,' he said. 'Only yesterday, Matron found it necessary to tell me that she found disquieting rumours going around, about you.'

'Nigel, you sound like a Victorian father reprimanding his daring young daughter.'

'I don't find it a matter for flippancy, Linda. That being your attitude, I must ask you to clear up, at once, this matter that is still unexplained, and rather unpleasant. The matter of the voice you were talking to in the upstairs hostel bathroom.'

'Oh, Nigel, for heaven's sake, isn't that over and done with long ago? It was back in March and everyone's forgotten it!'

'Oh, no. I haven't. I forget nothing that isn't cleared up,' he corrected me.

I got up. 'I'm going back to the hospital. If this is what is going to happen every time I come to dinner with you—'

'Well?' he asked dangerously.

I was going to flare out at him that I didn't have to marry him and that I would think twice about it. But that wasn't true. I knew in that moment that I wanted to marry him more than anything else. He infuriated me for being so suspicious, but then I could hardly blame him. The things I was doing were foolhardy in the extreme.

He wavered a little too, as he stared at me.

I think it was that which made me alter my tactics.

'Oh, Nigel, why are you so rotten and suspicious. Can't you trust me? You know what it's like in the hospital. We're kept hemmed in by thousands of petty rules and regulations, and we're always breaking them. It's just that I haven't got used to not breaking them, because I'm now in a different position to the others. I don't mean to embarrass you, but have a heart. I can't bear to be hemmed in like this.'

He came over to me then, and put his

hands on my shoulders.

'There … isn't anyone else, is there, Linda?'

It was the first time he had ever said it, and I saw that he, too, was jealous, but unlike David's jealousy, Nigel's was the insane kind all mixed up with suspicion and distrust. He couldn't help it. I suppose it was because of his sense of importance, and because it made him feel a fool.

'Of course there isn't!' I said, and let him take me into his arms for a moment.

He held me in a grip that hurt, but he didn't kiss me. He just stood with his lips against my hair, and looked down at the floor. I could see his face, reflected back again, in the mirrors. He wasn't satisfied even now.

'Then if there isn't anyone else, and you're just breaking rules like a damned silly schoolgirl, Linda, perhaps you won't mind telling me just who Alan Torringfield is.'

Chapter Sixteen

It was from that point, of course, that the situation deteriorated. I did my best, from the point of view of satisfying him that Alan Torringfield was merely a distant relative, but he had got his teeth into it, and wanted to know more and more, and if I was going to tell the truth, the whole thing would inevitably come out. If, on the other hand, I was prepared to tell one good straight lie, there the matter might end. But I couldn't be certain that it would. I couldn't be certain at that moment that I wanted to tell one good straight lie to Nigel or anyone else, about Alan or anything else to do with me. And anyway, I hadn't time. Nigel was waiting for his answer, and with each fleeting second, the situation became more tricky.

I broke away from him, and sat down again. 'Why did you ask that, Nigel?'

'Supposing you answer it first, and then you'll see,' he suggested.

I shrugged. 'I can't work out just what is the exact relationship between Alan and myself, but he's more or less haunted Marleigh Park, as far as I can remember.'

His eyes widened. 'Your aunt didn't

mention him!'

'Did she mention anyone else in the family, besides my father?'

'Naturally,' he said stiffly. 'She talked to me quite a lot about your family. I should have thought it odd if she hadn't.'

He sat watching me, with a curious look in his eyes, and as I didn't answer, he said again that he thought it was odd that Aunt Berenice hadn't mentioned him. It struck me that he probably thought that Alan was a complete stranger to her and not related at all. I decided to repair the damage.

'If you must know, Alan is the sort of relative most families have and prefer not to mention. She doesn't like him, and she'd give a lot, I know, to be sure she'd never see or hear from him again.'

'I see. And is Miss A Torringfield his sister?'

I had forgotten the parcel.

'He hasn't got a sister,' I said, pursuing the silly discussion still further. As always I was getting supremely irritated with all this, and I knew that it wouldn't be long before I flung all caution to the winds, and told him the truth, or flung myself out of the room – both courses leading to the same end. As I saw it at that moment, there was no other end.

And then Nigel went over to a small table, and took the wretched parcel out of a drawer. I recognised the thing a mile off.

He showed it to me, but still held it. 'I hate doing this, Linda, but if you will do strange things in this secretive manner, then you rather force my hand. The gate porter, on the occasion I mention, appeared completely put out when the so-called "visitor" went off in a hurry, at sight of me. He turned to me and asked me what I thought he ought to do with the package you had left for him. He was going off duty, and hadn't time to give it back to you.'

'And knowing you were my fiance he thought you'd do just as well,' I said, rather flippantly, because I couldn't think of any other attitude to adopt.

'Linda!' Nigel said, in as near a shout as he could bring himself to manage. 'For heaven's sake, don't be so trying! What *is* it all about? If the man is your cousin, why not send the thing to him through the post in an orthodox way (if you must send him packages) and not tell a cock-and-bull story about someone's man-friend, or whatever it was, to the gate porter, and to me!'

'It's perfectly simple, Nigel. You know all the rules and regulations. I couldn't post it to him because he's just moved, and I didn't know his new address. He could have written it, but Alan has a simple mind. He was passing and he thought he'd just drop in and ask me for it. But the rules won't permit that. That was why I ticked him off in the corridor for just coming in.'

'Why didn't you introduce him to me, instead of saying he was a visitor?'

'I hardly thought he was the type of relative you'd want to know about,' I said, coldly.

'And that was why you fabricated a story for the porter?'

'Oh, what does the porter matter?' I stormed. 'Why hold an inquisition of a small thing like this? Can't I send a parcel to my own cousin without all this?'

'What's in it?' he asked, turning it over.

'Mind your own business, Nigel!'

'It *is* my business,' he said quietly. 'If the man is really a black sheep, I shall want you to cut off all acquaintance with him. If he's really such an undesirable character, I naturally went to know what you could possibly want to send him, with such urgency. I think we'll open it.'

'Nigel! Don't you dare open that! Give it to me! It's mine, and you had no business to take it from the gate porter and keep it, like this!'

I tried to take it from him, but he held it out of my reach, his cold grey eyes boring into mine.

'I have to know all about it now,' he insisted. 'It looks very much to me as if the answer of the unpleasant episode is tied up here.'

I ripped off my ring.

That little action sobered both of us for the moment. 'Isn't that rather an admission of guilt, Linda?' he said quietly. 'Put it on again, before we get any further involved in this rather unfortunate scene.'

'Who started it?' I said, furiously. 'I'll put it on again if you give me back my package. You've no right to do this. I'm not married to you yet. I'm of age, anyway, and I still reserve the right to choose my own acquaintances. If that right is going to be taken from me, I'm not sure I want to put your ring back.'

'I don't think my wishes in that direction have been any secret to you from the start. But the matter has now gone further than that. The way you're behaving, and all this very strange air of secrecy rather suggests to me that this is something which must be looked into. It's beyond our little circle, Linda. It has to do with the good conduct of all nurses, and the prestige of the hospital. If you won't tell me what's in here, then I must assume that my guess was right. In that case, the package goes to Matron, if you won't allow me to open it.'

'I think you're crazy,' I said, after a pause. 'It's just something which Alan asked me to get for him. What's wrong with that?'

He turned the package over, as if he could make his eyes have X-ray qualities, and see within it. My heart was pounding unevenly, and it was all I could do not to snatch it from him and fling it into the fire or rush out of the house with it. It was so absurd, so tragically absurd. I had struggled so hard to get that money, to buy my own peace of mind, and now it was going to be the very instrument to destroy all my future. Such a small package, with so much destruction in it.

'It isn't a very convincing story,' he said.

I slipped down on to my knees beside him. 'Nigel, we're not ourselves,' I pleaded. 'Where are we going? If we're to be man and wife, can't we exercise a little trust? What does it matter to you about all this? Alan will soon be out of my life, and you'll never hear from him again. But if we're to have any happiness at all you mustn't – you *can't* – expect to know every little thing I do, every person I know or speak to, every thought in my head.'

I think he was a little insane at that moment, with jealousy and all the other attendant emotions. I realised, I think, at that precise second, that Nigel was the type to destroy his own happiness at any given time, because he couldn't trust those near to him. And yet I didn't mind. There was that strange fascination about him that drew me all the time, so that while in any other man I would have flung in the towel long ago, here I was persevering, excusing, turning a blind eye, pleading – anything, so that I didn't really have to close the door on a life of uneasy marriage with him. For that, I knew, was what it would be, all the time. Uneasy.

'What's in it, Linda?' he repeated.

I sat back on my heels, looking at him. I had been clutching at his hand, but I don't think he had noticed. It occurred to me then that he merely thought that Alan was my lover and that this was a small intimate gift that he wanted to unmask. I went a little mad I believe. A small voice inside clamoured, all right, let him see. Let him see.

I began to laugh, hysterically.

'My God, talk about Pandora's Box! You're worse than any woman, Nigel! All right, open it, if you dare – but heavens, how you'll be sorry!'

He ripped off the brown paper, and took off the little cardboard lid. Banknotes lay in all their nakedness, and on top my little note. *This is the last time.*

'Well?' I cried. 'Are you satisfied? Are you glad you looked?'

Blank astonishment was all over his face. He just didn't know what to do or to say. I watched him, wondering. I knew so little of him, basically, that I didn't know what he would do, either, and his final reaction was one that staggered me. He got up and swept me into his arms with one movement.

'Linda, Linda, you little fool! Why did you do it? Why didn't you come to me? Don't you know you don't have to do this? That there's protection for people from the Alans of this world?'

I thought he was quite insane, of course, and I looked warily up into his eyes.

'What idiocy have you been up to, to go to such lengths to keep it from me? Just let me get at the fellow and I'll give him the thrashing of his life, and then we'll turn him over to the police.'

Again, despite his sudden change of manner, and his fondling of me, he was waiting for his answer.

I couldn't cope with such egoism. When it sank into my head that it appealed to him that I had apparently had to go to such lengths just to keep some idiot prank from his knowledge, I was floored.

'It wasn't to keep it from you only, Nigel. It was to keep it from Matron, too. I happen to want to get my S.R.N. Alan was going to get me kicked out.'

I said it flatly. I said it knowing that I didn't have to say it. Even at that late stage, I knew that I could have pretended some prior romance with Alan, and that would have been all that was needed. Nigel would have been satisfied. If Alan, of course, had gone no further. But I was sickened of lies, of trying to keep all that misery at bay. Something in me clamoured to bring it all out in the open and be damned to the lot of them. And I wanted to deflate Nigel. Surely, surely, if he cared for me at all, he'd never want to let me go? David didn't.

Nigel said, 'Do you know what you're saying?'

I nodded.

'Then,' he said, slowly and deliberately, 'it might be as well if I had the whole story.'

I started talking. I found myself giving the bare, bald facts, and they sounded unreal in that unfriendly room. I recalled that on the occasion I had disclosed some of the things to David, I hadn't had to go into it so deeply. David had seen the newspaper reports. He had half the story already.

Nigel's face was wooden. I could see that he was hating every moment of it, and I felt sorry for him. When he had proposed to me, he had been so satisfied that he had found, for himself and quite without anyone's aid (least of all his old mother's) the perfect wife. He had said I was absolutely perfect, and that was a big admission for Nigel to make, and only possible because he was rating higher the credit for finding the perfect article than of my being the perfect article. Now, it was crumbling before his eyes.

'It was on the occasion of my twenty-first

birthday party,' I began. 'Alan was there, and a lot of young people pretty much like him. I'd been friends with them (against a dickens of a lot of family opposition) for four years. My father was all for not having them in the house, but my mother insisted that as I'd go around with them anyway, it was better to have them in the house than in someone else's place, not knowing who I was meeting.'

Nigel's mouth turned down. He didn't like that. Nor did he like the picture as it developed. It was like turning the clock back. I remembered it all so clearly, as if it were yesterday.

There were about eight or nine of us, in one of the smaller rooms, away from the big hall and the dancing. We were all rather merry, Alan particularly. He was talking some nonsense about me, and I couldn't be bothered to do anything about it. My head ached, and I wasn't enjoying my party a bit. Mother was ill, and hadn't been able to take any part in it, and my father was hating the whole thing.

Mother, who had been much more wealthy than my father, when she'd married him, had made her Will that day. The solicitors had been there, and she'd called me to her after they'd gone.

'Darling,' she had said. 'I wish you'd give up those wild friends of yours. It's aggravating your father so much.'

I had had nothing to say. She didn't know that I knew the truth about myself.

'You don't even have to be friends with Alan,' she had urged, tiredly. 'We would be happy if you didn't encourage him to come here.'

And still I had remained in wooden silence.

'We know the dreadful things he does,' she had said, saying things that obviously hurt her to say. 'We don't want him to influence you at all.'

And that had hurt dreadfully. It simply pressed home to me that she, too, was doubtful of my antecedents, and that if I had really been her daughter, she wouldn't have worried so much about Alan's bad influence.

'Well, I can't make you stop doing these things,' she had sighed. 'I do care for you so very much,' she had gone on, wishfully, 'and I do want everyone else to love you as much as I do, but you make it so difficult.'

The old lump had come into my throat, but still I couldn't speak, or make any offer to do as she wished.

'This is such an important birthday for you,' she had gone on, and told me what she was doing for my gift from her. 'And furthermore, I've settled your future for you, dear. They can't take it away from you, if you'll only be a good girl and do what we ask you.'

I think she must have been referring to the 'satisfactory marriage' which Aunt Berenice had so stressed. She didn't put it into actual words. I suppose she thought it wasn't necessary.

'I'm a sick woman, my dear, but if anything happens to me, your Aunt Berenice will look after you – if you'll only be good. You will do as she asks you, for my sake?'

'Does that mean give up my friends?' I had managed.

She had lay back then, spent, shaking her head. 'I could get well, I believe, if only these family upsets would stop. Your father – you – Alan – there isn't any peace. Oh, Linda, dear, why are you like this?'

I wondered what I would have thought of all that, if I'd still believed I was her daughter. Anyway, that bedside conversation ended in deadlock for us both, but it stayed with me all through the party, so that Alan's wild talk hardly penetrated my miserable thoughts. Only when my father appeared, looking about as angry as I've ever seen him, did it penetrate. And then it didn't make sense, just then.

'He was talking about my father not being such a saint as he made out, and a sneering remark about his 'adopting' me, which made everyone laugh,' I said to Nigel.

Nigel's face flamed, but he said nothing.

'As you can well imagine,' I said, 'if you know Mellingford Fane personally, he was the last person in the world to take such a thing lying down, even from a member of his family. In fact, I imagine he started his slander action against Alan with the greatest joy. He hated Alan.'

Nigel was still puzzled, I could see.

If it was my part in it which bothered him, he could have that too, I thought. 'Alan dragged me in, too. He said, after the case had started, that he was only voicing things I'd inferred myself. It was enough to make Mother insist on the case being stopped. She wouldn't have me dragged into it, and he knew it.'

I waited for Nigel to ask if it were true, but I saw it didn't matter to him. He just didn't care if I'd taken part in the whole rotten business or not. All he could say was, 'But your Aunt Berenice never told me – she deceived me into thinking–'

'Is she likely to have told you, Nigel?' I demanded, getting up. 'What does it matter – anything at all. The main thing is that I haven't got any parents. It was that sort of Home I was adopted out of!'

Poor Nigel. It was an affront to him that I was even in his home, let alone all the other implications.

I ripped off my engagement ring a second

time, and this time he didn't order me to put it back again.

'And it goes without saying, that I'll resign from the hospital,' I told him, stiffly. 'That'll save you the trouble of having me removed.'

That wasn't fair, and I knew it, but I was stung to say it. All my energies had been bent to prevent Alan from getting me out of hospital, and in the end it had been through Nigel.

Chapter Seventeen

As I packed my things, I reflected that this might not have happened if Frances had been here. We had worked as a team so well, covering up for each other. And then I thought, it couldn't have gone on. So long as Alan was breathing, there would be no peace for me.

I wondered where I would go, and what I would do. Since I had told Matron the bare unvarnished truth about my resigning, that finished the chances of my ever becoming an S.R.N. There was nothing else that I could do. Nothing that I wanted to do.

I took a room in a small hotel, and started answering advertisements for receptionists, things which didn't need any special training. I also tried to get Aunt Berenice on the telephone, to ask if I could go down to see her, but she was away.

David insisted on seeing me, so I let him take me to dinner. I grinned as he noticed that the big diamond was no longer on my left hand.

'I do drift in and out of the engaged state, don't I, David?'

'Linda, my dear, what on earth happened?

Do you really mean you resigned from the hospital?'

'I did. My fiance heard the whole disgraceful story, and unlike you, he couldn't take it.'

'But did that mean—'

'Oh, I suggested it myself,' I told him airily. 'I wasn't going to let him suggest that I stopped polluting his beloved hospital.'

'Want to tell me all about it?' he asked.

I nodded. I wanted, more than anything else, to talk about Nigel just then. I told David all about the package of money, too, and when he asked what had happened to Alan, I stared blankly at him.

'I'd forgotten about Alan for the moment,' I said.

'And your aunt?'

'She's away. I'll have to go down and see her, of course.'

'What will you tell her?'

'I don't know. I've never understood why she was so anxious for me to make a good marriage. I would have thought, after all that had passed, that she'd be jolly glad to see the back of me.'

'Perhaps, like me, she loved you for what you were,' David suggested softly.

'Aunt Berenice? I used to think so, but now I'm not so sure,' I mused. And then I realised what he had said, and I looked at him, and my voice was uncertain as I said,

'Did you really mean what you said, David?'

He shrugged, smiling.

'You're a disease, my dear. As long as I live, it'll be you, and only you.'

'I thought you weren't going to be able to take it, the first time I told you I was a foundling,' I said.

'Linda, are you still in love with Armstrong?'

Pain seared in me. I could only nod at him.

'Then it isn't any use, is it, asking if I stand a chance?'

'Would you want to, David, after all that's happened?' I gasped.

He nodded. 'Did you think I wouldn't?'

'But knowing I still love him?'

'I want to take care of you, Linda. But I suppose there's always a chance, if you stay free, that things will come right for you.'

I started to laugh, and he took my hand fiercely.

'Steady, Linda. Stop it.'

'It's all right. I'm not really hysterical. But if you could have just seen poor Nigel's face, while I was telling him. Oh, it was awful, awful. I don't suppose he's been so bitterly hurt in his life. To think that Aunt Berenice could treat him like that, as well as my part in it, that's what hurt him so.'

'What will you do, then?'

'Oh, I don't know. Get a job – that's if you'll provide me with a reference.'

'You'll need two,' he reminded me.

'Do you think Frances would–' I began, but he looked doubtful and that surprised me.

'Frances is expecting to become a mother. Evans is so damned protective, it's doubtful if he'd let her even hear of all this. You could try writing, of course.'

He didn't hold out much hope. I said I would write to her about the coming baby, and tell her how happy I was for her.

David said slowly, 'Evans will have heard about all this, you know,' and he looked at me as if he would have liked to say more but wasn't going to.

'You mean he won't let me get in touch with Frances?'

'I think he might feel a bit strongly on the subject. He's an odd sort of bird. Stuffy and all that.'

Stuffy was putting it mild. Of course, I reflected, if Frances were starting a line of holy little Evanses, then of course, he'd build a glass cage round her, and keep her in cotton wool.

'Never mind, David, I'll manage. Perhaps Aunt Berenice will do something.'

'Linda, do come and stay with us, if only for a bit. My people will love to have you.'

I shook my head fiercely, and then

remembered my manners and thanked him. He didn't press the point, but remarked, when at last he left me, that I knew where the Blakes lived, and that there were friends there whenever I wanted them.

Aunt Berenice requested me to go down the following weekend. I had a job in view, receptionist to a dentist, but he wanted all sorts of references before he'd start me. I went down to Marleigh prepared for battle.

The moment I saw Aunt Berenice, however, I knew that it was utterly useless to even mention the proffered job. She was a different person. I had never imagined she could be quite like this.

She did most of the talking, too. She told me that after all she had done to arrange that very important marriage, she was utterly astonished that I should behave in such a manner. She stressed the point that as I had been legally adopted, there was no need at all to dig out all that distressing business.

'But it wouldn't have been honest not to,' I pointed out. 'And besides, anyone could look the whole thing up if they wanted to.'

'Who is likely to want to, if they know nothing about it? Besides, the whole thing was hanging on the unfortunate person of Alan. If you hadn't given him money and done all those peculiar things, which I really can't understand at all, nothing would have been said, or thought about the matter.'

'But Alan would have seen to it–' I began.

And then she told me, to my utmost surprise, that she had been settling Alan herself. Alan, she said, would never have done anything at all. He was just bluffing me that he would, to get money out of me.

'But why didn't you tell me you were able to keep him quiet?' I protested.

'I am not used to having my methods questioned,' she said, icily. 'I told you you had no need to fear anything from him, but for reasons best known to yourself, you never seemed able to believe me. I wasn't prepared to do more. As it is, you've ruined your own future, and I wash my hands of you.'

'So you were keeping Alan quiet, and he banked on your not telling me, and worried the life out of me. He got away with it, too,' I marvelled. 'What I can't understand is, why you should have gone to so much trouble to get me married to Nigel?'

'I promised Mellingford's wife I would. Poor Elizabeth seemed so fond of you.'

She said it in such a tone as to suggest that she couldn't think why.

'I thought you were fond of me, too, Aunt Berenice,' I murmured, but she didn't answer me.

'Will you tell me if it was Nigel particularly whom mother wanted to see me married to, or just any rich man?'

'She didn't even know of Nigel Armstrong,' I was told.

'Then I suppose–' I began.

'I am not bothering to further another alliance for you,' she said, stiffly. 'I have gone to a great deal of trouble, only to have you smash up my plans, and once is enough. Remember, you took yourself off in a huff, and never let us know where you were, and only after endless trouble could I locate you, and also make the acquaintance of the most likely person to be interested in you.'

I had to admit that that was true.

'Aunt Berenice, there's one other thing. This money Mother left me. Why didn't I hear the Will read? Why wasn't I told about it before you did?'

She arched her eyebrows at me. 'You weren't supposed to know about it until your wedding,' she said. 'I told you as a special favour. It was the contents of a sealed envelope. The solicitors and I knew about it. I was to arrange the marriage, so your Mother gave me the details.'

'And she arranged something for you for your trouble?' I hazarded quietly. It was a shot in the dark, but by the angry glint in her eyes, I knew that the shaft had gone home.

'Where does the money go if I don't marry? Do you mind telling me that?'

'To the Orphanage,' she said, bitterly.

She looked at me then, and I knew she hadn't finished. She would work hard to find someone to take Nigel's place, when things had died down a bit, and she had smothered her anger against me. Because with great shrewdness my Mother had left enough, for that service, to make it worth Aunt Berenice's while.

She waited. I knew instinctively that I was the one who had to say the word, to beg her to overlook it, and to help me. Then she would graciously climb down, and tell me to stop being foolish about a job, make my peace with her brother and come back to Marleigh for another marriage to be arranged. They wouldn't let so much money go out of the family, I could see that. Aunt Berenice was a great one for saving face. All this time she had been paving the way for me to make a come-back, and to make it easy for my father to accept me back. He had thrown me out of the house before my mother had died, and so he didn't know the way she had bequeathed her property. She was the one with all the money, I recalled. And that was why I had been adopted, because it was her wish, and my father could only give way to his disapproval through the years in other ways. He couldn't prevent her wishes.

'I was going to ask you for a reference for

a job,' I murmured, thinking how when I had first seen Aunt Berenice today, I had thought she was finished with me.

She sat very still, thinking. I could almost hear her thoughts ticking over.

'Where is Alan at the moment?' she asked suddenly.

'I don't know. I haven't heard from him lately.'

'How much money has he had from you?'

I told her. 'Nothing since I was last here.'

She didn't mention all those lies I had told her. She brushed all that to one side as of no consequence.

'Don't give him anything else. There's no need to. Now you've made your disastrous exit from the hospital, there aren't any more threats he can make. So ignore him.'

'But supposing he–'

'Our solicitors are arranging to get him on to a rubber plantation. The idea isn't new, but it will keep him in money and out of the country. Now, I think the best thing for you will be to arrange a visit. Lady Herraleigh, I think that's far enough away, for a little while.'

I sat back. A fine show of anger, and then all the old machinery of arranging things. I was sick and tired of it all, and my temper, released from the old rigid bonds, flared out. I'd defeated her once, when I'd got myself into hospital to train as a nurse. I'd defeat her again.

'I don't want to be put out of the way, and then worked off as a desirable acquisition to some man's home,' I stormed. 'I just want a reference, to get a job, and be independent.'

She wouldn't quarrel with anyone. She merely raised her eyebrows, and did a nice piece of work, pointing out the discomforts of such a life, and the fact that I could carry out Mother's wishes and at the same time buy security, if I wasn't so pig-headed. As a last resort, she reminded me that as nothing was known of my real parents, she wasn't in the least surprised, whatever I chose to do.

If she thought that that last taunt was going to do any good, she was mistaken. On that note, I walked out, and I never went to Marleigh Park again.

I didn't get the job without the extra reference, but I still had the money I was going to give to Alan, and it lasted me quite a while. But of Alan, I saw nothing.

I got into the habit of searching people's faces again, as I had done during those early months in hospital. I missed nursing more than I could say, and I sometimes walked by Bardmore's, with an aching longing. If I hadn't resigned, I would be getting perilously near those finals.

One day I ran into Benny. She apparently knew nothing of my reason for leaving, and was frankly envious of my having so much time on my hands. When I got over my first embarrassment at meeting her, I took her to have a coffee. I wished I hadn't.

'I say, you know that fascinating chap who came in from casualties one day, and then came back as a gastric?' she began, and my heart turned over. 'Have you heard? He snuffed out – in Bardmore's, of all places! I think he must have liked us.'

'Alan Torringfield?' I whispered.

She nodded brightly. 'That's the name. You knew him, didn't you?'

I didn't answer that. 'What … how did he die?' I whispered.

'The police brought him in. He was hanging to the railings outside, and they thought he was drunk at first. He kept asking for someone. He said he'd got a whack on the head, and he kept shaking it. They patched him up in Casualties, but he didn't seem up to much, so they kept him in. I didn't see him, but Forbes told me about it. She was on duty on his ward. You know how he loved to talk about himself? He was telling her about a brawl he'd been in, in Soho, and he tried to get a message to you. He was absolutely staggered to hear you weren't there any more.'

'Go on,' I said, and tried to concentrate, but all I could think was, Alan was dead. If only I could have hung on a bit longer. Alan was dead. He couldn't worry me any more.

'Well, after a bit, he started shaking like a jelly, and bleeding from the ear. Forbes reported his rigours, and that got them a bit excited, but he was quiet enough afterwards. Then he just passed out.'

I thought she meant it was shock. Perhaps it was a shock that he'd lost touch with me. But Benny, completely cheerful and totally unimaginative as always, saw nothing in my silence, and went on: 'It was a brain injury, of course. Your glamorous playboy didn't do it. It was Ballard on at the time. Couldn't do a thing about it. Said he was past help before he was admitted to Casualties. I say, is it true that your engagement's all off? The good-looking Armstrong goes about wrapped in gloom. No more buckshee smiles for anyone.'

I got away from her as soon as I could. Funny, how synthetic life in the hospital sounded, once one was out of it. The old crushes on the good-looking honoraries, and the interest soon worked up in male patients like Alan, didn't even seem funny at this distance. I decided not to go near the hospital after that.

My stock of possible advertisements had been exhausted. I had tried everything, from companions and private nursing, receptionists, telephone operators, anything that didn't require qualifications beyond my range, but all needed references, and I had only one. Finally, my money almost ran out, I took to jobs which didn't need anything at all but a bit of nerve. Waitress jobs, baby-sitting, daily helps.

David ran into me about that time, and as always he looked at my hands, and I had to tell him what I was doing.

'What on earth does it matter?' I asked wearily. 'I never have to do the filthy jobs I had to in hospital, so who am I to complain?'

'You look ill, Linda. Why don't you come home for a bit?'

There were two reasons why I couldn't do that. One was that they would want to know where I was living, and I would be ashamed to tell them, and the other was that I probably wouldn't be there very long, if I couldn't scrape up enough for rent that week. In addition, there was a reason which David had partly guessed. I was ill, and I believed I knew what was wrong with me.

I said irrelevantly, 'I heard the other day that Alan is dead.'

I was surprised and disappointed to find that David knew of it already. I guessed that Frances had heard of it. She would, of course, from Gordon. It had been an interesting injury.

He went on talking, and I couldn't concentrate, because of the pain in my side. I tried to remember when it had started, but all mental effort defeated me. I was glad when he left me. I just wanted to crawl back to my horrible hard little bed and lie there, and wait till oblivion came. I was so hungry, and yet I had felt too sick to eat the good food David had brought me.

I walked unsteadily from the restaurant, without remembering how or when I had said goodbye to him. It was dark, and the streets were rain-washed, but it wasn't raining then. I thought I heard David's voice saying something about calling a taxi, but it couldn't have been. I was alone. People surged by me, and seemed to be coming straight at me, and I couldn't make my legs move to steer me out of their way. And then my legs seemed to crumple up, and pain envelope me, and darkness clamped down over everything. Out of the roaring dark-ness, came voices. I couldn't make sense of it at all, for the predominant voice was not David's, but Nigel's.

Chapter Eighteen

It was a long time before I knew what had happened. When I was at last able to understand things, I was astonished to recognise the familiar beige and cream paintwork of Bardmore's and the green and white striped dresses of the nurses coming in and out. The green checks of the student nurses, and one memorable day, Matron swept into my little ward, with its two unoccupied beds, one on either side of me, and spoke a word or two to me on her routine round of the hospital.

So I was back in Bardmore's after all, but not as a student nurse. I was a patient, and in those early days of consciousness, I couldn't remember what had happened to bring me there.

It was the strangest experience, lying there with the honorary and his 'firm' standing round me. The usual idiotic questions and answers, and I was the guinea-pig. Little by little I pieced together that I had had appendicitis, but that I had left it too long, and it had nearly been my finish, because the appendix had been difficult to get at, lying a little behind the bowel tract. There was something else, too, which I couldn't find out from anyone.

Benny came in to see me sometimes, and kept me au fait with what was going on in some of the other wards. It was somewhere to go during short time off, especially when the weather was too bad for her to go out.

Once Gordon Evans had occasion to come in, and he spoke to me, briefly. Very briefly. He didn't like me at all, I could see. He told me that he hadn't mentioned any of this to Frances, as she was expecting her baby very shortly.

My most frequent visitors were David and his family. They never failed me. Mrs Blake knitted me things, and David's father sometimes came in alone and read to me. I was too exhausted to make the effort myself, and I was frantically bored. He loved travel books, and criticisms, and was often surprised when the visiting hour came to an end.

One day Aunt Berenice swept in. She had come up by car, and she wore her mink coat, and dwarfed the little ward even more than Matron's presence had.

'I've only just heard of all this,' she said, disapprovingly.

'Didn't Nigel tell you?' I asked her.

'Nigel! Does he know of it?'

'Aunt Berenice, he operated on me. He saved my life,' I said, in some exasperation.

It shouldn't have been necessary to tell her that. It was so easy to find out who the surgeon was.

She sat down deliberately, kissed me graciously, and began to talk with me. First, she told me how furious she had been when she couldn't trace me, the last time I had left Marleigh Park. It was unreasonable of me, she averred, unfair, unkind, considering how much I meant to her. She went on to tell me that my father had decided to have me home again. He had been very sorry about the estrangement, she said. Now that Alan was dead (she didn't seem to think it necessary to mention how she knew of that) then bygones could be bygones.

After the visiting hour was over, Aunt Berenice went about arranging things, with her usual gracious air and steamroller tactics. She arranged for my removal to a nursing home, she chose a place for my recuperation, and arranged also for a private nurse to be engaged. She by-passed Nigel in everything, which of course upset him terribly, and she also by-passed the Blake family – though whether she knew that, I didn't know. Probably not.

Nigel came to see me the next day. He shocked me. He looked so different. Benny had said he went about wrapped in gloom, and I saw now just what she meant.

'Are you ill, too, Nigel?' I asked faintly.

'No, Linda,' he said, sitting looking at me.

'You look – not a bit like you,' was all I could manage.

And when he still didn't speak, I said to him, 'Thank you very much for all you've done. It must have been very tiresome for you, and very bad luck that you happened to be on op. theatre duty at the time.'

His look was a strange one.

'I wasn't, you know. Don't you know how it all happened?'

I shook my head.

'Those good friends of yours, the Blakes, were the cause of it. They took you to their home when you were ill, and called in their own doctor. Through him, they specially asked for me to do the job.'

'And you didn't feel you could refuse?' I murmured.

'I wanted to do it,' he said tightly, and looked down at his clasped hands.

'I would have understood if you hadn't,' I marvelled.

'Young Blake – he's a nice chap,' Nigel said.

'Yes,' I agreed.

'He'll take care of you,' he said.

'You know he loves me?' I murmured.

'It sticks out a mile. I only wondered whether you knew it yourself, Linda.'

I closed my eyes. It wasn't any use. David had been so good to me. I owed it to him, to admit the truth behind his present kindness.

'I was engaged to him once, Nigel, before I met you.'

He looked surprised, and then angry. 'Did you throw him over for me?'

I nodded. 'He knew I didn't care for him that way. He offered to release me.'

His anger was short-lived. There was something else on his mind, and it was pushing David out, I could see.

'Linda, did you have a very bad time, after you resigned from Bardmore's?'

I was at once wary.

'Oh, not too bad,' I said.

'Where did you live?' he persisted.

'Here and there. Hotels, mainly. Why?'

'What sort of hotels?'

'What sort of hotels would you think I'd frequent, Nigel?'

'Ordinarily, pretty good ones. But you'd cut off from your family again. I can't think what you did for funds. Low, weren't they?'

'I had the money in a certain package,' I said, flicking at him savagely, because I resented what I considered to be sheer prying.

That hurt him, and even in my low state, it gave me some satisfaction.

He tried again. 'I think you must have suffered awful privations. You got into a bad state of health.'

'Anyone can get appendicitis.'

'You got something more,' he told me, looking up at me then. And I saw pity in his eyes.

'What else?' I whispered, and I felt that every atom of strength in me was draining itself away.

'You have to go to a sanatorium,' he said, quietly. 'You know what that means? It's only just started, and if you'll do as I ask, we can stop it, given time.'

'T.B!' I whispered, and I was appalled.

He nodded.

'No, oh, no, there wasn't time! It was only a few months. I did pretty well at first. I– Well, I economised on food but it was summer and–'

Nigel said, gently, 'If there's a family history of it, time doesn't matter. Just the given conditions, that's all that's necessary to start it off.'

'Family history,' I whispered, and stared helplessly at him.

'We just don't know,' he repeated.

He took my hand.

'Linda, will you let me take care of you? I know just the man for the job. I have every faith in him. His place is–'

'No! Why should you? I don't want your charity, Nigel!'

'It isn't charity,' he said, his face curiously drawn. And then, still holding my hand, he put it to his face, and ducked his head down.

I said, not understanding, 'Isn't it a good thing, Nigel, that we broke it off before all this came out. What a wife you'd have landed yourself with. And you thought I was so perfect!'

He looked up again at that, as if surprised that even in my weak state, I could keep lashing at him.

'That was my error,' he said, and his face was ashen. 'I put too much importance on the perfection of the thing, and I forgot my own feelings. I happened to be in love with you, too, but I never remembered that until it was too late.'

'Too late?' I repeated.

'Too late for us. Unless you feel you can start all over again? But of course, I suppose it's Blake after all, isn't it?'

'Start all over?' I repeated, in dazed fashion.

'I could do so much more for you than Blake can, good fellow that he is. Linda, let me, my dear.'

'Haven't you forgotten the salient facts that caused our poor little affair to break up at first, Nigel? I'm not fit to be the wife of a surgeon?'

He didn't answer, and I could see that that was still a stumbling block, which he was at the moment trying not to look at. I imagine he was wanting to look after me, as only he could, and that he wasn't going to think of what would happen once I was well again. That would take care of itself.

'If you really want to help me, give me a reference. I can't get a job with only one,' I said, clinging to the one thing I had been wanting madly before I was taken ill.

'A job?' he asked, blankly.

'Receptionist,' I told him.

'You're not fit to work,' he said, and in such a tone that I interpreted the meaning aloud.

'Not ever again?'

He shook his head. 'We'll see,' he said, as an afterthought.

'Nigel, Aunt Berenice came yesterday. She made a lot of arrangements. Did you know?'

He smiled wryly. 'It wasn't possible not to know.'

'Well, did she know about … this development?'

'I imagine so,' he agreed.

'Then why?' A thought struck me, and I said suddenly, 'Nigel, did you know I had quite a lot of money coming to me if I married you?'

Again that glowing anger, as he said, 'I'm not a poor man myself, Linda.'

I supposed that to mean that my having money didn't mean much to him one way or the other, but I would have preferred it if he had said so, or denied that he had known about my money. I sighed, and left the argument alone. I was terribly tired.

He left me then, with nothing settled. I suppose he had it in mind to take it up another day. I was sure he never thought I'd fall in with Aunt Berenice's wishes and let her whisk me away under her care.

But I did. I did it during that long sleepless night, because I didn't want to see David and his people again. They evidently felt, kind souls that they were, that I was now alone and in their care. They must have known, too, that the business of getting me well again was beyond their purses. David was rash enough to take anything on, or should I say that he was kind enough? He would take it on, if it bled him white, that I knew. And I couldn't do it.

Neither could I let Nigel take up the old threads again. I didn't say so to him, but I didn't believe that he loved me, and I knew that I still loved him. I couldn't risk all the months, probably years, of watching him pretend a love for me that wasn't there, just for the sake of getting me well again. If anyone was going to work on me, for the sake of conscience, let it be Aunt Berenice.

I left Bardmore's before Nigel came to see me again. When Aunt Berenice moved, she moved quickly. I didn't go back to the Park, but straight to a sanatorium overlooking the Channel. It was a lovely sunny day in early December. The sun sparkled on the sea, and the air was keen and good. All my windows were open, and I was put out on to a balcony overlooking smooth lawns.

I wrote a letter to David, and explained to him a lot of things that had been on my mind even before I was taken ill. I told him, as best I could (and words weren't my strong point) how I felt about obligations and old ties.

It wasn't a nice job, and I stumbled over it a good deal, crossing out sentences, whole passages sometimes, but at last getting it pretty near to how I wanted it.

'I know, my dear, that your feeling for me is as real as it ever was, and that to you I am still in the same position as I ever was. And that naturally you will want to be responsible for me now I am helpless. But have you thought of how I feel? I think I'd rather die than know that every penny of your hard-earned money was going out on me, especially as no one will give me any guarantee that I can be cured. David, I beg of you, my dear, forget me. I'm not worth it.'

That was how I ended. Not a very nice letter for any man to receive, I suppose, but I did so want him to know that, before it went any further. Better that, I reasoned, than to have him run the risk of thinking that now I was alone, I might come to love him, or at least feel I needed him.

No, better cut it off, then and now.

Just before Christmas, Aunt Berenice came to see me again. She was her old gracious self, and told me fondly that I was so much better now, that she had really felt she couldn't let things go on any longer without talking to me about them.

'I still have my promise to your dear mother weighing on my conscience,' she smiled, and 'conscience' seemed an odd word to come from her. 'And I know just the person she would have wished to see you married to.'

'I'm not in a fit state to be married,' I protested faintly.

'But you will be. Sooner than you think, if there were the money to pay for special treatment, dear.'

'Who is it?' I asked tiredly.

'Do you remember Gil?'

I made the required effort, and recalled a sickly youth who had been introduced to me as the nephew of the other sister. The sister of Mellingford Fane and Aunt Berenice. A hawk-nosed woman with cold black eyes, whom poor Mother disliked, and I think, rather feared.

'But he hasn't got any money,' I said, bluntly.

'But he has a title, dear, and that, I imagine, would have pleased poor Elizabeth very much. She did so want to see you *secure*.'

That money again. They weren't going to let it go to the Orphanage if they could help it. I wished, in that moment, that I knew how much it was. I was very curious, the more Aunt Berenice worked for it.

'Why didn't you think of him before you thought of Nigel Armstrong?' I asked.

She didn't like being questioned. She flushed pink and sat looking past my left ear until she was composed enough to answer me.

'Gil was engaged to someone else at the time,' she admitted.

'Wouldn't she have him?' I grinned, knowing that Aunt Berenice would consider that question in very bad taste. 'You know, Nigel asked me if we could go back to where we were, and I've a great good mind to do that.'

She looked so put out that I decided that Mother must have left me more money than I realised.

'Is there a certainty that I shall get well?' I wanted to know.

'If you go to Switzerland for a certain treatment that has just been discovered,' she said, slowly, watching me, 'there is as much certainty as can be.'

'What does that mean?'

'Really, Linda, I don't see why you can't take my word for it that it is certain, without all these questions.'

But I wouldn't. I approached the doctor, and he told me a far different story.

I lay all night thinking, in the uncomfortable knowledge that Aunt Berenice was staying at the nearby hotel, waiting for my answer. I knew that if I consented to go to Switzerland, she would take the precaution of having me married to the loathsome Gil. I turned over in my mind the few people I had with whom I could discuss this frantically important matter. The question which the doctor had left for me only to make up my mind about. There was Nigel; there was Frances, and her Gordon, or at the worst, Gordon alone. I know he would had advised me, even though he did experience dislike at the sight of me. And there was the Blake family; David, his mother and his father.

I lay there staring blankly at the ceiling. It was the first time that I had ever ached for David. It was no use making lists of other people, and fooling myself all the time. It was David that I wanted. Not only to talk to and ask his advice, but to feel that he was beside me, mine, in this vital point of my life, and like a fool I had burnt my boats with that wretched letter. I had sent him out of my life, just when I needed him most.

Chapter Nineteen

Aunt Berenice went back to Marleigh Park furious with me and with everyone else. I told her, at last, that I couldn't make up my mind. It was the only way. I knew she wouldn't wash her hands of me, not while there was breath in my body to say the 'yes' which she so ardently wanted. I didn't know what had happened to her nephew Gil or his precarious finances, to make her suddenly think up this mad scheme, but it must have been something bigger than the termination of his engagement, and something much more imperative. I couldn't recall much about him, except a hazy recollection that he gambled. It was probably his own racing stables that were doing such damage to his purse.

I settled down to a pretty bleak Christmas. I didn't think that the Blakes would know where I was, and so I wasn't surprised when, on Christmas Day, I had no gifts or mail from outside the sanatorium. Other patients, and some of the nurses, remembered me, but that wasn't quite the same. There wasn't even a word from Frances.

And then after breakfast, my nurse asked

me if I'd take a London telephone call.

I thought at once it was Nigel.

She said, 'He specially asked if you'd care to speak to him, before he was put through. It's a Mr Blake.'

'David!' I said weakly, into the receiver. 'How nice of you to–' and then the conventional remark broke off in mid-air. I couldn't go on.

'Linda, don't cry, dearest. I've only just heard where you were. Why didn't you put your address on your letter?'

'Didn't want you to know,' I managed.

'I couldn't let Christmas go by without–' he began.

'David, I wanted you,' I said without thinking.

There was silence on the line for a moment, and then he shouted: 'Say that again!'

'I wanted you,' I said. 'I wanted you so badly and I couldn't write, not after that letter–'

I forgot most of that incoherent conversation, and I don't recall what I did with the rest of the day. I lived for the next day, and on Boxing Day David came.

I said, painfully, 'Don't come too near me.'

It was a terribly moving visit. I wouldn't go through it again for anything in the world. Most of the time, we just sat trying to keep a hold on our emotions, before we could go on talking.

David put down a load of parcels, and letters from the family and during awkward spots in the conversation, he told me about them, and delivered verbal messages.

'David, have they told you anything? About me, I mean?'

He said, not looking at me, and keeping a terrific control on his facial muscles, 'Linda, dearest, I know just how ill you have to be, to be here.'

'I see,' I said, and I couldn't go on, either.

He had been with me for some time, before I could tell him what I wanted. I said it badly, and watched him for reactions because I had thought about it so much, turned it over in my mind so much, that it was all distorted, and I could only see it the way I wanted to.

'David, there's a – an attempted cure – I think they'd call it. I would have to go to Switzerland.'

'What would it cost?' was his first question, and I could almost see him adding up every future penny he was ever likely to make, just to put it at my disposal, without question.

'There isn't any charge, they say. I'd sort of be a guinea pig. You see, I might die. Or the cure might come off, but set up something else. They don't know. It's a gamble.'

I couldn't look at him. I went on, desperately, 'Half of me wants to take the risk, half of me is dead scared. But it's better – anything's better – than this living death. Oh, David, talk to me about it. Tell me to go.'

It was wicked to torture him with such a decision. I wished, watching him, that I'd never asked him about it, never asked him to come at all.

Because the tension was so horrible, I plunged into telling him about Aunt Berenice and her plan, and the money, and the whole wretched business of the marriage she had planned with Nigel.

'She wanted you to go to Switzerland, not letting you know the risk?'

I nodded. 'Well, I suppose so. I expect she found out all she could about it first. I'm not sure, of course, but she was so angry when I wouldn't make up my mind either way.'

'And letting you think she was paying for it?'

I nodded again.

'Have you spoken to Armstrong about it?' he asked.

'No, David, I don't want to. I didn't want to talk to anyone about it, but you. Only you.'

'Why, Linda?' His question was barely audible.

I lay back and looked at him. Afterwards,

he told me that my eyes were like stars, but I didn't know that then. I only knew that all that I had ever experienced, either for Alan or Nigel, was only synthetic. For David, I had come a long way, and found, still without fully appreciating it, love for him, and still I only experienced fully a great need.

'You want me to make up your mind for you?' he whispered.

I nodded.

'All right,' he said. 'You've loved life so much, I can't advise you to count the risks. That would be condemning you to stay here for ever.'

His voice broke and he gathered me into his arms. 'I love you so much,' I heard him say, in a muffled voice, 'I'd rather know you were dead, than staying here.'

'But David, it isn't just dying. That isn't the only risk. Remember, I might still be an invalid, from something else.'

I listened for his reply, and cherished it, all the way to Switzerland, and all through the distinctly unpleasant treatment I went through.

David came with me, and lived nearby, still writing, and mailing his stuff to England. It was Spring before I could even try to get about again, and then I knew that I'd only be a shadow of my former vigorous self.

I remembered the thing he had said to me, that Boxing Day in England, when we were being married at the little Protestant Church, so far away from home.

'I'm the sort of chap who wants a woman to need him,' he had whispered. 'You've always been so self-reliant, my dearest, but now, heaven help us, it's changed. Remember, my darling, always, I'm here. Always here. Only let me look after you.'

And because my emotion was engulfing me, I had tried to laugh, saying, 'Fine way for a nurse to finish up. I'd dedicated my life to looking after other people.'

And David had said, prophetically, the thing I think I had always wanted to hear: 'Not any more, Linda darling. I'll care for you.'

This Large Print Book, for people
who cannot read normal print,
is published under the auspices of

THE ULVERSCROFT FOUNDATION

... we hope you have enjoyed this book.
Please think for a moment about those
who have worse eyesight than you ...
and are unable to even read or enjoy
Large Print without great difficulty.

You can help them by sending a
donation, large or small, to:

**The Ulverscroft Foundation,
1, The Green, Bradgate Road,
Anstey, Leicestershire, LE7 7FU,
England.**
or request a copy of our brochure for
more details.

The Foundation will use all donations
to assist those people who are visually
impaired and need special attention
with medical research, diagnosis
and treatment.

Thank you very much for your help.